# BELOVED LEAH

## Cynthia Davis

Americana Publishing Inc.
303 San Mateo Blvd. NE
Suite 104A
Albuquerque, NM 87108

ISBN  978-1-58288-220-8

# AMERICANA PUBLISHING, INC.

## AUDIE AWARD WINNER
### BEST NEW AUDIOBOOK PUBLISHER 2001
### AUDIO PUBLISHERS ASSOCIATION

---

To request a catalog or to order books and audiobooks
from Americana Publishing, please call or visit our website.

## www.americanabooks.com

Titles from other publishers are also available
through AmericanaBooks.com.

---

Americana Publishing, Inc.
303 San Mateo Blvd. NE, Suite 104A
Albuquerque, NM 87108

Thanks to my sisters in Christ – Becky Thomson, Gay Crouch, Bethany Spratley, and Christina Leonard – for their unconditional love. And thanks to Ken, Julie, Joyce, and Ruth for their encouragement.

# Author's Notes

**Gen. 29:20** *So Jacob served seven years for Rachel, and they seemed to him but a few days because of the love he had for her.* [21]*Then Jacob said to Laban, "Give me my wife that I may go in to her, for my time is completed."* [22]*So Laban gathered together all the people of the place, and made a feast.* [23]*But in the evening he took his daughter Leah and brought her to Jacob; and he went in to her.* [24]*(Laban gave his maid Zilpah to his daughter Leah to be her maid.)* [25]*When morning came, it was Leah! And Jacob said to Laban, "What is this you have done to me? Did I not serve with you for Rachel? Why then have you deceived me?"* [26]*Laban said, "This is not done in our country--giving the younger before the firstborn.* [27]*Complete the week of this one, and we will give you the other also in return for serving me another seven years."* [28]*Jacob did so, and completed her week; then Laban gave him his daughter Rachel as a wife.*

**Gen. 30:25** *When Rachel had borne Joseph, Jacob said to Laban, "Send me away, that I may go to my own home and country.* [26]*Give me my wives and my children for whom I have served you, and let me go; for you know very well the service I have given you."* [27]*But Laban said to him, "If you will allow me to say so, I have learned by divination that the LORD has blessed me because of you;* [28]*name your wages, and I will give it."* [29]*Jacob said to him, "You yourself know how I have served you, and how your cattle have fared with me.* [30]*For you had little before I came, and it has increased abundantly; and the LORD has blessed you wherever I turned. But now when shall I provide for my own household also?"* [31]*He said, "What shall I give you?" Jacob said, "You shall not give me anything; if you will do* *this for me, I will again feed your flock and keep it:* [32] *let me pass through all your flock today, removing from it every speckled and spotted sheep and every black lamb, and the spotted and speckled among the goats; and such shall be my wages.* [33] *So my honesty will answer for me later, when you come to look into my wages with you. Every one that is not speckled and spotted among the goats and black among the lambs, if found with me, shall be counted stolen."* [34] *Laban said, "Good! Let it be as you have said."*

Eleven of Jacob's twelve sons were born in the seven years after his marriages, first to Leah and then a week later to Rachel, and at the time, Laban agreed with Jacob that all the spotted and striped animals that were born were his wages. Jacob served Laban for another six years before leaving Haran. He was in Haran a total of twenty years. When he left he was a rich man with wives and children and servants.

## JACOB'S SONS IN ORDER OF BIRTH:

| Year of marriage | Leah | Rachel | Zilpah Leah's maid | Bilhah Rachel's maid |
|---|---|---|---|---|
| First | Reuben | | | |
| Second | Simeon | | | |
| Third | Levi | | | Dan |
| Fourth | Judah | | Gad | Napthali |
| Fifth | Issachar | | Asher | |
| Sixth | Zebulon | | | |
| Seventh | Dinah | Joseph | | |

Jacob's youngest and twelfth son, Benjamin, was born between Bethel and Hebron at Ephrath (Bethlehem) where Rachel died and was buried.

# Prologue

"Rachel, Rachel," the dying woman muttered through lips that barely moved.

The two serving women glanced at each other across the pallet of blankets and pillows piled on the tent floor. One bent to moisten a cloth in the bowl of water. She pressed a few drops between the parted lips. "Mistress." The other maid smoothed a few straggling strands of gray, wiry hair off the wrinkled forehead. The skin beneath her fingers felt like a piece of papyrus left too long in the desert sun. A single tear slid down her cheek as she thought of the many times the now frail hands had served the suffering and frightened in the family.

Outside the tent, the women could hear the deep voices of men gathered around their father. His voice came heavily through the tent flap. "God of my fathers, again you take away from me one I love."

A moan distracted Bilhah and Zilpah. They turned to minister to their beloved mistress and friend. She tossed her head fretfully and again called for her sister. She was far away in the past. The woman she sought was buried near Ephrath over twenty years earlier. "Rachel, where are you?" Again the cry was wrenched from fevered lips.

"Dear mistress," Zilpah spoke soothingly, "Rachel is not here." The old woman lay quiet while the maid chaffed her hand to bring warmth into the cold fingers.

In the silence, Jacob could be heard pleading with his God. "You came to me on the way to Haran, my God, and promised me prosperity. You took away Rachel at Ephrath. Joseph, the son of your promise, you stole from me at Dothan. Now, Leah, mother of my sons lies dying. What good are riches without the ones I love? God of my Fathers, I will be left desolate when I bury Leah in the cave with Abraham and Sarah and my parents."

"My father," young Benjamin's voice was heard, "you will not be alone."

"My son, someday you will bury the one you love above all else, and your life, too, will be empty." Despair was in the deep voice.

"Surely you have not forgotten that your God has restored Joseph to you." Again Benjamin tried to comfort the old man.

"Yes, if God is gracious and allows me to live to see my son," he responded dolefully.

In a rustling of movement, the tent flap was pushed aside. The warm breeze flowed through the opening and brushed across the woman on the pallet. She roused to call again, "Rachel!"

"Hush, my wife." Jacob knelt and took Leah's hand. "Rest and be well. Rachel is not here. We will travel together to her son. I need you, do not leave me."

The woman tossed her head restlessly and opened her eyes. They softened when she saw the man kneeling beside her. She seemed to return to the present from somewhere far away. His eyes filled with tears as he caressed her weak hands. "My husband," her voice was gentle. She tried to lift her one hand to touch the man's face. "I never understood," she murmured.

"Leah, you are the strong, faithful woman I am honored to call my wife." The old man kissed the hand he held. "Your belief in the One God has strengthened me in the darkest times. I need you now to go with me to Egypt. Together we will find our son."

A slight smile crossed her lips as she reminded him, "Rachel's son, my love." She took a deep, ragged breath. "I never understood your love for Rachel. Through all her childless years and whining, your devotion remained strong. I was angry and bitter for I thought that you had nothing left for me. The God of your Fathers has taught me that love can be boundless." Her head moved fretfully against the pillows, and Zilpah hurried to adjust them. Bilhah brought a cup of water. Gratefully, the woman drank.

Slowly, she turned her hand in her husband's to take a hold of his fingers, and then looked at him with pleading eyes. "Jacob, my husband," she continued her confession, "my venom taught our sons to hate their brother. God has shown me that He has forgiven me, for Joseph is restored to you. Your God has taught me that even such grievous fury as mine can be forgiven."

Tears trickled down the old man's cheeks and he kissed her wrinkled cheeks. "Leah, beloved Leah," he whispered, "you, too, have I loved."

With great effort, the woman feebly touched the cherished face behind the graying beard. She sighed, "I know that, now. All I ever saw was Rachel loved by our father and then by you for her beauty. Never could I believe that I was lovable. My jealousy poisoned my sons against their brother. When you see Joseph, ask him to forgive me."

She fell silent while the man wept unabashedly. Then, she closed her eyes and drifted off into a doze before she open her eyes again. "Call my sons." Her voice was stronger and laced with urgency. "I must tell them to let go of their hatred before it consumes them as it did me."

At a nod from Jacob, Bilhah went to the tent flap and ushered in the eleven waiting men. Zilpah helped her mistress sit up. Jacob leaned against the mound of pillows, cradling his wife in his. She seemed to gain strength looking at the big men that she bore and raised. "My sons, hear my story," she said looking at each face in turn. "Give up the anger you hold in your hearts against your brother. It will only destroy you in the way it consumed my relationship with Rachel."

Reuben, the firstborn, leaned forward. His mouth opened on a denial. A slight shake of his mother's head stopped him.

"Hear my story," she repeated. "It was always Rachel who was adored by everyone. She received special attention because she was lovely and pleasant. I was envious and my hostility grew."

The men crouched around the pallet while Zilpah held the cup of water for Leah to take another sip. Then she began her story.

# Chapter 1

"Rachel! Rachel!" I looked out the door. No one was in the street in either direction except a couple of boys chasing a puppy. "Where is that girl? She is never here when I need help." My question was directed to the serving girl standing in the kitchen. Her answer did nothing to ease my frustration.

"I think she has gone to help with the lambing."

Not trusting myself to speak, I snatched the tray of sweetmeats from the girl. My thoughts were angry as I tromped back to the room where my father sat with his friends. Once again my little sister had managed to slip away when there was work to be done. Not that our father, Laban, ever insisted that she take her woman's place and learn to cook and weave, no, he was too proud of her skill with the flocks and herds.

"Leah, don't you see that her work with the sheep and goats is important?" Often he tried to make me see that she was working.

"She plays with the lambs," I argued. "She should be here, learning woman's things." I was hurt that my father didn't notice my efforts to keep his home neat and clean. It was my feet that stood for hours at the market haggling over the best price. My hands ensured that food was prepared and on the table when he and my brothers came in from the fields. When my mother died, I uncomplainingly took over running the household. It was Rachel, though, that got the praise for her games with the animals.

Again and again I approached Laban. "Rachel is getting too old to be alone in the fields with the men."

"Her brothers are there." He patted my shoulder. "No one will harm her. Soon she will be a woman and then she will have to stay in the house with you. Losing her mother was hard on Rachel. She needs to have this time with the animals."

I turned away to hide the tears in my eyes. My mother's death had been hard on me, too. I remembered Miriam smiling indulgently at the little girl toddling among the lambs. Even then I had argued, but both parents had laughed indulgently and encouraged her. Now, I was sure that even my mother would insist that Rachel should be acting more like a woman. She was ten, and soon the men would begin to look at Laban's youngest daughter with more than casual interest. All too well, I knew that my own square body would never attract the interest that Rachel's long legs and slender figure would. Leaving the men to their meal, I strode back to the kitchen. Angrily, I twisted my limp black hair up onto my head. I had a constant battle just to keep it neat. It had a bad habit of straggling around my face. Rachel, of course, had glorious wavy auburn hair. Everyone commented on it. The only thing people noticed about me were my eyes. It was a small comfort that my mother had often told me that my gray eyes were windows into my soul. "Your heart can be seen in your eyes, my daughter," she said whenever I complained that Rachel was prettier. "Like me, you care and love deeply. Those feelings shine from your eyes. Few people are so blessed by the gods." For a year after she died, I stared into her bronze mirror daily trying to see if there was any difference in my eyes now that my heart was broken. I gave up, finally, when Rachel caught me at it and teased me about

being vain. Still, I couldn't help overhearing the whispers of
the girls at the well. "Leah is angry today; you can tell by her
eyes." Or, "I wonder why Leah is sad today." It was
embarrassing to have everyone know how I felt just by
looking at me. The emotions had shown from my eyes even
when I smiled and talked about the weather. Now, I rarely
looked anyone in the face, preferring a sideways glance while
pretending to be occupied with filling the water jar or passing
a tray of food. A tear of self-pity threatened to fall as I paused
to stare out the slit of a window that let in some light and air,
but kept out most of the wind and weather. Beyond my view,
I imagined that Rachel and the shepherds were lazing in the
spring sun. The snow still clung to the mountain heights, but
the valleys were greening with fresh grass for the animals.
That was especially good for the ewes with new lambs,
Rachel and my brothers insisted. They added that the flock
would double this year if the weather stayed fine.

Rubbing my stinging eyes with the back of my hand, I
continued into the cool, windowless pit dug down into the
ground. Here we stored the wine and cheese to keep them
fresh. I selected a skin of wine and retraced my steps to give
it to my father.

"Where is your sister?" My father's question stopped me at
the door.

"With the sheep." I hoped no one would hear the bitter
gall in my throat.

"Of course." His jovial laugh told me that Laban, at least,
didn't notice. "I should have known. My youngest daughter is
almost like another son. She is so good with the sheep."

I didn't want to hear the rest of his praise of Rachel. My
bare feet slapped hard on the dirt floor as I stormed back to
the kitchen. The hospitality in the house of Laban would not
be compromised, even if Rachel wasn't available to help. The
serving girl helped me arrange the wooden platters of meat,

vegetables, and bread. We carried them into the room. Deep in conversation, my father barely nodded when I set them down. "You may go, I'll clean up," I told the surprised girl when we returned to the kitchen. With a grateful smile, she slipped out the door. I knew she had a sweetheart among the village boys and would hurry to his side with her unexpected free time. "I don't care," I told myself, pouring the scraps into the bucket for the chickens. "I don't need a sweetheart. My job is to take care of Father." No one saw the salt tears that fell onto the pans while I rubbed them clean with sand.

As spring was followed by summer, then fall and winter, all of Sumeria and Haran believed that the gods kept the cycles in order year after year. An, Enlil, and Enki, the triple gods of creation, maintained life by keeping the heaven, air, and water in balance. Im-dugud, god of storms, was welcomed and feared. Welcomed because the rain and snow made the land green, but feared because his rages brought about terrible destruction. Together, Inanna, the winged goddess of love, fertility, and war and Nanna, the moon god, brought strife and peace to men, women, and families. I wasn't sure that I believed in the many gods; but, like everyone in Haran, we had a family shrine for the gods that we hoped would bless us. Laban favored An and Inanna although we also had a statue of Im-dugud, with his lion-head, for protection against destruction.

On festival days, we all trouped together to the massive temple that was located in the center of Haran. Only the priests could climb the steps to the top of the ziggurat, where the ceremonial altar stood. It was there that sacrifices were made and religious ceremonies performed. Inside the temple were statues of every faithful person in the town. In that way, a constant worshipping presence was assured, and the gods were more apt to bless us all. I remembered my grandfather, Nahor, telling me that to the south, in Nippur and Ur, the ziggurats were bigger and taller and looked as if they were reaching to the heavens. As a little girl, I couldn't imagine anything grander than the temple dedicated to Inanna in Haran. It was the only structure in town decorated with colored cones arranged in geometric designs all around the sides. Even now, at thirteen, I was sure that Haran was the best town in the world.

Sometimes I wondered if it would be any different if there really was only one God like Abraham the Wanderer had insisted. Abraham was my great uncle, brother to my grandfather. Sometimes in the winter evenings, and when Rachel asked, our father would tell us stories about Abraham. He told how Abram, as he was known, had traveled with his brother, Nahor, and their father, Terah, from Ur far to the south. They had all settled here in Haran, but Abraham was restless. He was driven by the belief in the One God that he insisted met him in Ur. Endlessly, he claimed that he was promised a land of his own. I never understood the compulsion that drove this childless man to travel back and forth from Haran to Canaan to Egypt and finally to settle in Canaan. He maintained, despite years of no children, that this god promised him many descendants. Rachel always pointed out that he did finally have a son. Isaac was born when Abraham's wife was nearly one hundred years old. Too old for children, so it must have been a miracle, Laban's voice always ended the saga with the same singsong words.

So, the seasons slid into years. Rachel's twelfth birthday came and went. Still she spent her days in the fields with the men and flocks. I wondered if I was the only one who saw that the child was becoming a woman. It was no surprise when she slipped into bed with me early one morning, eyes wide with some emotion. "Leah! Sister!" she whispered, tugging my arm.

Drowsily I mumbled something.

"Sister, I think I have become a woman!"

I sat straight up on my mat of skins and blankets. "What?" I must have spoken loudly for she put her hand over my mouth.

"Hush, I don't want Father to know. He won't let me go with him to sell the sheep today if he finds out."

"You'll need the rags." Ever practical, I dug out a supply of the monthly cloths for her.

"You cannot go with Father today." I made the statement fully expecting an argument. Instead she threw herself into my arms, sobbing.

"I don't want to be a woman and be shut away for a week at a time once every moon turning."

Awkwardly, I patted her back. Even as a baby, Rachel had been so self-assured she never wanted the hugs I had desperately wanted to give her. Now, I gathered her slender form into my hungry arms.

"There, there, sweet sister, it isn't so bad. This means that Father will begin to look for a husband for you."

"I don't want a husband," she wailed, forgetting to be quiet. "I want things to go on as they were. I want to tend the sheep and go with Father and ..." Another sobbing fit robbed her of words.

The curtain was pulled back. Laban stood in the doorway rubbing his eyes. "What is the problem?"

Before I could answer, my sister flung herself at the man. "Say I may still go with you to the market!" Her words were tinged with hysteria.

"But, why? What?" His eyes sought mine over her head. I suppose he thought I had been scolding my sister. His hand stroked the auburn hair that rippled down her back.

With a shrug, I held up the monthly cloths and said, "Rachel has this night become a woman."

The emotions that played across the man's face almost brought a smile to my lips. His fatherly love fought with the lifelong cultural training that said the girl in his arms was untouchable at this time. "My daughter." As gently as he could, he disengaged her arms from his neck. "You are now a woman and must begin to act the part of an adult. This is a great night. We will celebrate your coming of age."

I took her slender form into my arms again. "It's not fair!" Rachel sobbed over and over. "I don't want a Feast! I want to go to the market with you! I want to go to the fields! I don't want to be a woman and be married!"

With a last look at the two of us, Father backed out of the room. He shook his head as he considered the turn of events. Perhaps it was the first time he realized that he had two marriageable daughters to deal with. I knew that the men of Haran would waste no time petitioning for Rachel's hand. I wondered who would be found for me. It is the law of Innana, the goddess of love, that the elder must be wed first.

Rachel and I spent the day together. Gradually she became calm and we talked about womanly things. I was surprised at how much she appreciated my taking over the role of mother and homemaker. "I could never do all that you do. The daily baking and cleaning and washing would make me crazy," she confided.

"You'll have to learn so you can do all these things when you have a husband and children," I reminded her.

"No." Stubbornly she shook her head. "I plan to continue to watch the sheep. You don't need a husband to be a shepherdess."

I shook my head since I was sure that even our doting father would insist that Rachel act the woman's part now. To divert the conversation, I started planning the celebration of her womanhood. She couldn't resist the idea of a party in her honor with the new tunic and the trip to the temple for a special sacrifice.

"You will see that being a woman is not so bad," I coaxed. Because she quit arguing, I thought she finally agreed to give up her idea of being a shepherdess.

During the next week of excitement, ritual and revelry, I tried not to compare the elaborate ceremony to the simple one-day observance of my coming of age.

"My mother had just died," I explained when a new slave girl, Zilpah, asked me about it one day as we prepared yet another banquet for the endless party. Rachel was in her element with the local girls attending her and leading her into the dances that were such an important part of the celebration. A hard knot formed in my heart, though, when I saw the young men staring at my little sister. I saw several of them approach Laban but in each case he shook his head. Eagerly, I looked forward to the end of the week when Rachel would take her proper place with me in the household duties.

Rachel got her way, of course. I don't know how she convinced my father, but except for one week each month, she was allowed to be in the fields with the sheep. The men of Haran stopped petitioning Laban for her hand. I tried to ignore the whispers from the older women when I went to the well and market. Each of their words was a barb that sank into my hardening heart. "There she goes, Laban's oldest daughter. Such a shame, her father can't marry her to anyone."

"Do you know? The little sister is exiled to the fields until he can find Leah a husband."

"Rachel is so lovely, there would be no problem getting her wed."

"My own Abdam asked to make her his wife."

"I heard even the son of the chief, the *Gal,* has approached Laban."

The shearing was complete and the summer heat was starting to set in. I overheard my brothers talking to my father. "We must start using the well tomorrow. The *Gal* has spoken. The brooks have dried up until the later rains come, Im-dugud willing." It was Joshih who spoke.

Laban nodded. "That is good. This is the time of alliance among all the flocks and herdsmen."

Cabel, my oldest brother laughed. "We have to help each other. That stone over the well is too heavy for any one man to move."

As I listened, I remembered my one visit to the flock well. It was called *Gal-beer* because only the chief of Haran could order its use. I remembered my father telling the story of how it was first dug by his grandfather when he came to the area. "He saw that the land was rich and the hills offered protection. So Terah settled here with his sons, Abram and Nahor, their wives, and his grandson, Lot. He called the name of the town Haran after the son who died in Ur. Terah and his sons dug this well so that the animals would not suffer or need to be driven far in the heat of the summer. When others settled in Haran, the stone was put in place as protection against misuse." It was a monstrous slab of rock that covered the top. Father explained to me that the stone kept the well closed until all the flocks were gathered. In that way, no one could steal extra water for his herds. The huge boulder took two or three strong men to move it. The drawing of the water into the troughs took extra time. The men would not want food until after dark.

It was rather nice to have the extra time to prepare the evening meal. I told Bilhah and Zilpah, the serving girls, that we could wait until the shadows started to lengthen and the air began to cool before preparing the food platters. We talked about many things while listening for the sounds of feet and the mixed baaa-ing of sheep and goats as Rachel brought them into the nightly enclosure.

The lions, bears, and wild dogs in the hills made it unsafe for unattended flocks to be out at night. Many shepherds slept with their animals in the fields, but Laban had wisely forbidden Rachel from doing so. Only during the week when Rachel wasn't allowed to be in the fields did Joshih and Cabel watch over all the animals and keep them in the fields at night with their own animals.

"It is too much trouble to sort out your flocks from ours and bring just some into the fold," they argued, and Laban agreed.

"Until the gods send a husband to watch the flocks, Rachel will watch my animals with her brothers' help."

"Pray the gods send a husband speedily," Joshih joked.

I added my prayers to his because, surprisingly, no suitor had come forward for Rachel. At least none that I knew of. Without the possibility of Rachel's betrothal, I knew I had no chance of ever being married. Perhaps it was her easy, friendly way with the men or the fact that they looked on her as a comrade and not as a bride. Maybe Laban was too cautious in his views on a husband for his beloved baby. For whatever reason, Rachel remained happily unattached.

One hot day I looked up from my kneading trough, pausing to wipe the sweat from my forehead and tuck a straggling hair back behind my ear. What I saw made me jump up, my heart leaping in fear. Rachel was running full speed down the street. "Father, Father!" I heard her voice. She did not sound frightened, just excited. I relaxed slightly even as Laban rushed past me.

"What is it? Where are the sheep?" His eyes scanned the road behind her.

She caught his hand, panting and impatient. "At the well. Listen, the most amazing thing has happened!"

I left my bread to join the group. "Come inside, you are making a scene," I urged. Curious faces were appearing in doorways up and down the street. My mind could already hear the whispers and titters at the well in the morning. Every woman in town already thought Rachel was scandalous for being a shepherdess. Now, this display of unseemly behavior would add to their gossip.

"Come inside." I tugged her arm. She shook off my hand angrily and turned to Laban.

"You don't understand! Father, your sister Rebekah's son has come."

"Rebekah!" I saw my father's eyes grow soft remembering the little sister who went to the wild unsettled land of Canaan to be the bride of Isaac, the miracle son of Abraham the Wanderer. Sometimes he talked about her strong will. He compared her beauty and spirit to Rachel. "Like you, my daughter, your aunt Rebekah knew what she wanted. When Abraham's servant came seeking a bride, she didn't hesitate. Eagerly, she agreed to go with him back to Canaan. She told me that was what the One God wanted her to do because she was the one who answered Eleazar's prayer at the well."

In my heart I admired her courage. Going off into the wilds to marry a man she had not even met took bravery. That she believed the strange One God of Abraham wanted her to wed Isaac was even more amazing to me. I wondered what her son was like and why he was here now.

"Rebekah," Laban repeated, "has a son?"

"Yes! He is here! Now! At the well!" Rachel punctuated each sentence with a tug on her father's arm. "Come and meet him! He rolled away the well stone so the flocks could be watered. He kissed me," her eyes grew wide as she spoke, and dreamy as her hand rubbed one cheek, "and called me his beloved cousin!"

"I must go and welcome him!" The man started rapidly up the street with Rachel dancing beside him.

They left me standing in the middle of the street. With a proud lift of my head, I ignored the curious eyes that now focused on me. Outwardly calm, I turned back to my house. My hands and teeth were clenched tightly. I allowed myself a brief moment of anger and smashed a vase of dead flowers against the wall before walking to the kitchen. Bilhah and Zilpah were waiting; eyes wide with unanswered questions.

"It seems that we will have company for dinner." The calmness of my tone surprised even me. "Our cousin from Canaan has come. We have much to do." I began outlining things that needed to be done. "Bilhah, you clean and straighten the main room. There is a broken vase to be picked up." The girl hurried to her task. "Zilpah, see that fresh water is drawn to wash our guest's feet." She grabbed a jar and scurried off to get the water. "I will see about a festive meal. There are plenty of vegetables and the bread was just ready for the oven. Fortunately, the lamb was prepared yesterday." Muttering instructions to myself, I patted the bread into shape and slid it into the round oven outside. Then I set about slicing meat and vegetables. Soon Zilpah, then Bilhah, joined me. In the silent camaraderie of women performing urgent tasks, our hands flew. Just as we heard Laban's voice and the animals in the enclosure, we put the finishing touches on an elegant meal. The bread, piping hot and nicely browned, was piled on a tray at the last minute.

"Here we are, son of my sister." I heard my father's voice echoing through the house. "Let me welcome you into my humble home. Here is water to wash the dust of travel from your feet and hands."

"My lord uncle is most kind." I heard a pleasing voice reply.

"Come, be seated. I am sure my daughter has some fine feast prepared to honor your coming."

I heard a note of awe in the visitor's voice. "Rachel, my cousin, has prepared a feast also?"

"No, my older daughter." Laban clarified the situation. It was my cue. I turned to pick up the tray of bread and nearly ran into Rachel. How she had managed to pen the flock, wash her face and hands, change her dress, and comb her hair in order to be standing in *my* kitchen, holding *my* tray of bread was a mystery I never solved.

"I'll take that," I hissed, anger mounting at her presumption.

"I just want to help." Her lips formed a familiar pout and a tear glistened in the corners of her eyes.

"Then bring the wine," I ordered. "It is my place, as elder, to take the bread of hospitality." For a minute I thought she would argue, but then she shrugged and took the jar of wine from Zilpah. Gracefully, as though she carried it everyday, she balanced the jar on her shoulder. It made me angrier to see how womanly she looked. Her gown flowed around her figure so easily, and her hair glistened in the glow of the lamp. I swallowed hard and led the way to where my father and cousin reclined on cushions. The serving girls followed with the meat and vegetables.

My first sight of Rebekah's son made my head whirl and my knees shake. I understood Rachel's sudden helpfulness. To say Jacob was handsome is to say that the Euphrates is a steam. From his brown curly hair to the broad shoulders and gentle smile above the thick beard, he was perfection. I carefully set the bread down in front of my father and lowered my eyes hoping no one noticed my stare.

"Jacob, you have met Rachel. This is my elder daughter, Leah."

I wished he hadn't made it sound like I was ancient and past hope. Belatedly, I realized that unlike Rachel, I had not had time to change my flour-spotted dress. My face, too, no doubt had flour streaked across it, and I knew my hair was straggling around my face, as usual.

Gallantly, the man rose to embrace me. "Cousin Leah, I had no idea that I would find such a welcoming family here in Haran. Here, I find my uncle and my two cousins, the beauteous and friendly Rachel and Leah of the lovely eyes."

"Welcome to our home," I managed to whisper above the pounding of my heart. He had noticed my stare. I hoped that my admiration hadn't been too evident in my eyes. "We will leave you to your meal."

Rachel hesitated before following. I thought she was going to beg to stay with the men. Instead, she gave a graceful salaam and trailed after me to the kitchen.

# Chapter 2

Bilhah and Zilpah watched in amazement as Rachel danced around the center of the kitchen. She caught my hands and dragged me into her dance. "Leah, my sister, is he not the most handsome man you have ever seen?" She let go of my hands to caper outside. The setting sun lit up the eastern hills with the glow that foretold a calm night. On an average night, Rachel and the flocks would just be returning. Tonight, our animals were safely penned and I heard the sound of the few other herds that were driven in for the night.

"The gods are gracious," she announced to no one in particular. "I have prayed for a husband who is not like these local herdsmen."

"Has he said or done anything to make you think …" I started the question feeling the all too familiar vise of jealousy tightening around my heart.

My radiant sister spun back into the room with a laugh. Oblivious to my pain, she skipped over to light an oil lamp. "How could he? We only just met." Her laughing eyes looked into mine. "But, he will talk to Father. I can feel it."

Her assurance took my breath away. Too stunned to even scold her for the conceit, I watched my sister skip outside. She made a slender and graceful figure as she raised her arms in praise to the gods who seemed to listen to her prayers while ignoring mine.

"You are the eldest," Bilhah's voice reminded me. "Surely your father will do nothing until you are wed."

"Then there is no hope for either of us to have a groom," I muttered the words under my breath, but followed them with a desperate cry to the gods from my heart. Inanna, goddess of love, send me a groom. Ninhursag, mother of all gods, the eldest must wed before the younger daughter. Don't let me be shamed by Rachel's marriage."

The image of Jacob, son of Isaac and Rebekah, came into my mind as I prayed. I rejected that thought as impossible. He had called Rachel beauteous and only in passing noticed that I even had eyes. He did call them lovely; my heart reminded me as I stared at the rising moon.

The next few days sped by. Rachel resumed her shepherdess duties. Laban and Jacob were seen together all around Haran. My father seemed genuinely fond of his nephew. At the well, all the young girls could talk about was our handsome guest.

"Leah, how lucky you are to have such a cousin."

"Is he really from the wild Canaan?"

"He can't be from Canaan. Everyone from there is wild, smelly, and uncouth!"

"Have you seen Leah's cousin? There is nothing uncouth about him!"

"Will he still be here for the harvest festival?"

I answered or nodded as required. It was odd to be the center of attention. For the first time in my life, I was almost accepted as one of the group. For the moment, they forgot that I was 'poor, odd Leah with the beautiful sister'.

Nothing was said about how long Jacob would be staying, so I could not reply to the eager questions about whether the young man would be in Haran when the harvest was gathered in. My curiosity was as great as the rest of the town. I planned to ask Laban. Then, I overheard a conversation that made it unnecessary.

I returned from the well to hear Laban's question. "Tell me, my nephew, why did Rebekah really send you here? Surely such a trip away from family is not usual. Are you in some trouble in Canaan?" Jacob cleared his throat and I imagined him looking down as he pondered how to answer. He didn't respond immediately. "My son," the man urged, "we are kin. It is best to tell the truth."

I almost laughed because it was well known that of all men, Laban son of Nahor could twist the truth to his own advantage like no one else in Haran. Rarely did I remember a time when someone had taken advantage of him. Without actually lying, he could make you believe you heard one thing when he really meant another. Many a trader had come off second best in dealings with my father. There were countless examples of others coming out on the short end of a bargain without quite understanding how it happened.

My cousin again cleared his throat. I gently set down my water jar and stood quietly in the hall near the niche that held the family teraphim. Finally, he said, "My twin brother Esau believed that I stole his blessing from our father Isaac. Mother felt it best that I leave the area until he cooled down. So she sent me here to Haran on the pretext of finding a wife from her brother."

My father burst into gales of laughter. I heard him slap the young man's back. "A man after my own heart! Tell me, how do you steal a blessing?"

"Well." I heard the hesitation in Jacob's voice as if he were half ashamed. Then he plunged ahead. "My father, Isaac, is blind now in his old age. He sent Esau to hunt and prepare a dish of wild meat so he could bless him before he dies. Mother overheard the conversation. She has always considered me the favorite. There was a prophecy given to her when she was pregnant. The seer told her 'you carry two nations in your womb. The older shall serve the younger'." He paused and sighed, "Anyway, she prepared a seasoned stew for me to take to Isaac. We tied skins on my arms for Esau is a hairy man. I was afraid that my father would grasp my arms and discover that I was trying to trick him. Mother gave me a robe of my brother's to wear. So, my father believed that I was Esau and gave me the blessing of the firstborn."

Jacob stopped and I realized that I had been holding my breath. Laban laughed again. "What a story! What a sister! She is a credit to this family! Tell me, what happened when your brother returned?"

"Esau came in from the hunt, prepared the food and took it to Isaac. I heard my father's keening cry when he realized what had happened. That hurt me worse than his rage would have." I could hear the sorrow and remorse in my cousin's words. "Esau stormed out of the tent. He was in a rage. I think even my mother was afraid of him at that moment. If he had met me, I would not be here today."

He stopped, but Laban continued to prod. "Then my sister convinced her husband to send you away. She told him you should get a wife from her people." He chuckled, enjoying the bizarre humor in the situation. "Didn't the man know the real reason?"

"Probably." Jacob defended his father. "Like my mother, he saw it as a good excuse to get me out of Esau's sight until he forgot his wrath."

Again my father laughed. I should have stopped listening then, but as I picked up my jar the words came clearly to me. "I would not like to make my sister a liar. I believe you have found in this house one you would like for a bride." Laban's voice was still jovial but I heard the bargaining edge slip into the intonation. "No need to blush, my boy. I have seen your eyes following her. I have noted the way you slip out to help with the sheep in the afternoons."

The vicious claws of jealousy grabbed my throat. "It is not fair," I screamed inside even as I heard Jacob's reply.

"Yes, my lord uncle, it is true. Rachel is in my eyes and in my heart, since the first moment I saw her coming to water your flocks."

"There is a problem, my son."

I had started to turn away again but Laban's words stopped me, gave me hope. Did he remember that he had an older daughter yet unwed? Would he propose me as the bride?

"Uncle?" Jacob seemed confused.

The next words dashed my hopes. "You have brought no bride price with you." I wondered what trap my father was setting. The smug sound of his voice warned me that he had a plan.

"True, my uncle, I left in such haste that there was not time to prepare and bring such a necessity." The young man's voice sounded dejected.

"Do not despair." His voice changed as Laban crossed the room. I could imagine him gripping Jacob's arm in a friendly way as he continued. "We can work out something. I would rather see my daughter wed to a kinsman than to one of these local men." My father was silent, as though thinking. "Of course." I heard his hands clap together, giving the impression of a great idea striking him. "It is quite simple. You will work for me to earn your bride!"

"I don't understand." Things were moving too fast for my cousin. I felt a moment's sympathy. When my father was negotiating nothing stopped him.

"It is simple. Rather than insisting on payment of a dowry, you will work for," I heard the smile in my father's voice and, in my mind, I saw the ingratiating grin he used when

persuading someone to slip into the neatly set trap, "say ..."
another masterful pause, "seven years for your bride."

"Seven years?" Jacob seemed stunned.

"Surely love is worth seven years of your life." The tone
implied that the man couldn't understand the hesitation.

"Yes." The young man still seemed uncertain.

"You will care for my flocks and herds. I have often
wished I had a trustworthy son to keep them in the fields at
night. Cabel and Joshih are busy with their own beasts. Now
the gods have provided, or perhaps it is the One God your
father believes in. It is the perfect solution for both of us.
Don't you agree?"

"Yes, Uncle." Jacob seemed more sure and I felt a tear
trickle down my cheek as my hopes slipped away. My father
had bought seven years free labor with the promise of Rachel.
That meant he had seven years to get me wed first.

"Let us drink to our agreement. Later, we will make it
public. Leah, are you here?" Laban's voice grew louder as he
crossed toward the doorway. I barely had time to scurry to
the kitchen and attack an onion before he pulled the curtain
back. "Daughter, bring a jug of wine. Your cousin and I have
an agreement to seal."

"Yes, Father." I hoped the strong smell of the onion
explained my choked tones.

Before I carried the wine in, I splashed water on my face
and eyes. Still, I knew they were red rimmed from the tears. I
didn't dare look at my cousin. The misery in my heart would
have been too obvious.

"You must rejoice with us, my daughter," Laban said.
"Jacob has agreed to work seven years for me to earn a
bride."

I think I said something appropriate before I fled back to
the security of the kitchen. When Bilhah and Zilpah returned

from the market they found me feverishly chopping onions and radishes.

# Chapter 3

For me, the seven years dragged by. Each turning of a season brought closer the inevitable shame of having Rachel married before I was even betrothed. It wasn't that Rachel didn't try to interest the men of Haran in me. She thought up some excuse for me to accompany her to every festival. I never realized there were so many. The shearing followed the lambing feasts. Then there were feasts for the success of each planting, and in the fall came the harvest festival. Each month there was a festival to the moon or some god.

"Leah, you must come. What will the gossips say if Jacob and I are at the harvest festival without you? Besides," here my radiant sister danced around, "a new merchant has come to town. A rich catch for the daughter of Laban, son of Nahor."

When I shook my head at her antics, she continued. "You must come and wear this new gown. See how the rich embroidery brightens your cheeks."

She held up the gown and shoved me to the bronze mirror. In the lamplight, the brilliant colors did almost make me pretty. In laughing at my sister, my gray eyes looked almost happy.

"This is to wear as your bridesmaid." I pushed away the thought that someone, maybe even Jacob, would find me attractive in the new dress.

"Silly," she laughed as she tugged my serviceable brown tunic over my head. "I'll get Father to purchase you another length of cloth for my wedding. It isn't until spring, anyway. You can't hide away during the last harvest festival I will attend unwed."

My sister slid the soft new material over my head. Then, with gentle hands, she arranged my straggling hair. Somehow she fluffed it until I was amazed at the transformation in the mirror. Leaving me staring at my reflection, she hurried into her own festive gown. I saw her drag the wooden brush briefly through her thick waves of hair. A couple of shell embellished combs held it back from her face. They were bought from traders from the coast. With a brief glance in the mirror, she took my hand.

"Come on, let's go show Father and Jacob."

I saw Laban frown when he saw what I was wearing. Rachel intervened before he could say a word. "Doesn't Leah look lovely tonight? It was foolish to leave this gown bundled away. See how the embroidery brings out her beautiful eyes."

In the face of such enthusiasm, which left me blushing, the men were speechless.

Jacob smiled at me briefly, "You do look very nice, cousin." He turned to gaze at Rachel with an entirely different smile.

"Well, then, come along." My father gruffly led the way.

The new dress gave me confidence, which gradually ebbed away as the festival continued. Despite a brief conversation, I could see that the new rich merchant was much more interested in pursuing the youngest daughter of Abiram, the *Gal.*

Rachel left me to my own devices after dragging me into the circle dance of celebration. My feet refused to cooperate.

I seemed to be going left when everyone else was turning right. As soon as I could, I slipped out of the circle.

The evening was entirely ruined when I overheard two of the shepherds talking. "I saw Rachel's sister here tonight."

"Her father is anxious to see her wed before Rachel. Watch you don't stand too close or Laban will have you matched with her."

The loud guffaws and coarse comments made me cover my ears and back further into the shadows so I wouldn't hear anything else.

Father must have heard something, too. Several times over the next few weeks, I caught him staring at me with a considering expression. It made me nervous. That look usually meant he was planning something.

* * *

Winter that year was bitterly cold. The flocks were brought in early every night from the meager grazing. When the snow came, the animals were fed on the hay that was stockpiled each year.

Laban and Jacob both refused to let Rachel go out in the cold with the sheep. We spent the time weaving blankets and sewing useful things for the time when she would have her own home. The men used the warmer days to put the finishing touches on the house next door where the couple would live.

Daily the girl grew more excited. "Only two more moon cycles until spring," she told me one morning as she watched a full moon set in the west. "The second full moon after this will see me a bride!" She hugged the linen material to her breast. Father had bought the fine yardage from traders on their way from Egypt to the holy city of Nippur where the gods met to decide the fate of all Sumeria. I knew it cost dearly, but nothing was too good for Rachel.

I missed a stitch in the embroidery that would ornament the gown. My eyes blurred for a moment with tears of self-pity.

Rachel saw and misunderstood my emotion. "Dear Leah," she knelt beside me, "you are so sweet to do this fine embroidery for me. I know it makes your eyes tired but I shall treasure it all the more for the love you put into it." Her hand covered mine. "Don't cry, I shall still be near, you know. We do not plan on going back to Canaan anytime soon."

"You have talked of that to Jacob?" I asked, my voice sharp to cover the hurt in my heart.

"We talk of everything," she sighed happily. "He tells me of the tents where he grew up. They are so different from here where the houses are sturdy and immovable." With a smile, Rachel stared off into space imagining the tents she would someday see and live in.

"Often he tells me of the One God that he believes in."

"Isn't that strange?" I asked. It was something I always wondered about. "How can anyone choose just one god when there are so many different things? There has to be a god for each blessing or curse doesn't there?"

The girl shrugged, "The way Jacob explains it, the One God is all blessing. His God even promised to bring him back home while he was on his way here." She paused and then added, "I don't care what god he worships as long as Inanna has given him to me as husband."

The men's voices interrupted our conversation. Rachel's eyes sparkled and she swiftly folded away her work. I stood up and went into the kitchen.

Late that night, I lay awake thinking about a god who only gives blessings and promises good things. The gods of Haran had to be constantly propitiated with sacrifices for fair weather or for rich harvests and peace. Still, I was never sure that any prayers were heard. The god of Jacob and Abraham the Wanderer seemed like a friendlier god.

Hesitantly, I prayed, "One God, if you are real, as Abraham the Wanderer and Jacob say you are, then send me, I pray, a groom that I may not be shamed here in Haran by Rachel's wedding. My prayers to the gods of my family have not been heard. If you are real, hear me now." I suppose I expected some miraculous occurrence—a man pounding on the door demanding me as wife, perhaps. Nothing happened at all until Laban called me to him just before Rachel's big day.

"Walk with me to see how the snow is melting," he suggested.

In amazement, I stared at my father. "I am in the middle of making the foods for Rachel's wedding feast!" I held up my sticky hands as evidence.

"That will wait," he stated. "Wash your hands and come with me."

Shaking my head over the fact that men didn't understand wedding preparations, I went to wash. Obediently, I walked beside him toward the fields. Snow still hid in the shadowy crevasses and on the heights. Lower down, the ground was warming and beginning to show a hint of green.

"You are my elder daughter," the man remarked after we walked in silence for several minutes.

"Yes," I replied when he seemed to be expecting an answer.

"You should be wed before your sister," the statement was out. Said plainly and openly. I felt the knife-like pain of jealous anger I thought I had contained.

"Yes," my answer was barely audible.

"You will be wed before Rachel." His calmly stated words stopped me in my tracks.

I stared at my father as if he had suddenly grown two heads. We stood on the path. His height meant I had to tilt my head back to look at him. I know my mouth was open in surprise. When I said nothing, he took my arm and tucked it through his.

"Leah," he began persuasively, "I would not see you hurt. I have a plan."

Somewhere in the back of my mind a warning tried to be heard. I was too interested in what my father's plan was to pay it any heed.

"Yes?" It was a question and I held my breath for the answer.

"You, not Rachel, will marry Jacob."

For the second time I stopped and stared open-mouthed at the stranger who looked like my father. "How?" I managed to croak the word. My thoughts were a tumbling turmoil of hope and fear, joy and desperation. Was this how the One God answered prayers?

"It is simple, really." The man was so pleased with the solution he didn't see any complications. His enthusiasm carried me along as he explained. "The bride is veiled and not uncovered until the couple is together in the marriage tent after the feast. I will see that Jacob drinks deeply and the rest is up to you."

My heart started pounding in apprehension but a wisp of hope swirled around in my head. Could such a trick work? I ignored the little voice that tried to warn me that no good could come of such a plan.

"Rachel is taller than me," I argued trying to find a flaw.

"The headdress is tall and you will be seated nearly the whole time."

"I wouldn't know what to say ... my voice is different from Rachel's." Sanity tried to assert itself even while my heart began to thud heavily and repeat 'it could work, it could work'.

"If you whisper and act shy, Jacob will not realize until too late that he has married my Leah and not Rachel." Laban crossed his arms and rocked on his heels in satisfaction. He smiled at me.

My eyes must have mirrored my conflicting emotions because he reached out to gently take my face between his hands. I was surprised at the kindness in his eyes.

"I do not want to see you shamed. I think you are not averse to the thought of Rebekah's son as your husband."

I felt tears gathering in my eyes as I nodded. "What of Rachel?" My voice was barely a whisper as I thought all too briefly of her anguish and anger.

"Let me deal with your sister," was the ambiguous reply. "Then it is settled." My father turned back to Haran. "You will be the bride in two days when the moon is full."

The walk back seemed unreal and the next two days were equally extraordinary. I continued with the feast preparations, but my hands would shake at inopportune moments. Bilhah and Zilpah teased me about having bride nerves for my sister. I tried to laugh, but it stuck in my throat.

The night before the wedding I stared out the door. The special tent was set up in the courtyard. Rachel came to stand beside me.

"Tomorrow it will all be different!" She exclaimed happily. Her face was aglow with joy.

"Yes," was all I was able to say. Impulsively, I drew her into my arms. "Little sister, I love you." It was the closest I could come to an apology for the planned deception. I turned to hurry away and bumped into Laban.

"Rachel, my child." His voice was gentle and loving. "You shall spend the night in the quiet of the temple praying to

Inanna for a fruitful marriage. I will take you there and come for you when it is time."

Trustingly, my sister put her hand in his and walked toward the towering ziggurat. I understood that the priests had been paid to keep her there.

"Tomorrow, all will be different," I repeated Rachel's words wondering if I had the courage to carry out Father's plan. My heart was thundering as I looked at the wedding tent.

The day dawned auspiciously clear. Zilpah came to me carrying the linen bridal gown. "The master said that I am now your maid. He said that you are the bride today." Her eyes were alive with curiosity.

"Yes, that is true." I managed somehow to talk around the lump of fear in my throat. Surely Jacob would notice something amiss. I was not at all like Rachel. The man would see and expose the deception. The end result would be worse than letting Rachel marry first.

Zilpah asked me no more questions. She concentrated on helping me dress in the bridal array. My hair was gently combed before the thick veil was draped over my head. Then the elaborate headdress was secured. Around my neck and arms, all the festive chains and bangles were fastened. Each ornament on the jewelry was a part of my dowry. My palms were painted with henna. When it wore off, the honeymoon would be over.

"You are a lovely bride," the maid said, stepping back to admire her work.

I stood still in the center of the room I had shared with my sister for the past seven years. Here we had come to understand each other's feelings. The deep watches of the night heard shared hopes and dreams. I knew my sister truly loved the man I was now marrying. I had no idea how Father planned to console her when she learned the truth. I raised my hand to remove the veil and headdress. Before I could complete the action Laban entered the room.

"The bride is ready?" The question needed no answer.

"Father," my voice was full of pleading, "I cannot …"

"Nonsense. Your chair and attendants await," his jovial tone did nothing to soothe my fears. I stood as though rooted to the ground.

"Such a shy bride." He picked me up, carried me outside to where to bridal litter and all the attendants waited. At his entrance, tambourines, bells, and pipes started their chorus. Joyful clapping and cheers from the watching neighbors only made me cringe in fear and guilt.

Before drawing the curtains on the litter, he whispered encouragingly, "Don't worry, it will be fine."

My whole body was shaking so much I could not have walked if I had to. The procession set out through the streets. Jacob with his groomsmen met us in front of the ziggurat. With tears in my eyes I looked at the temple and wondered where in the structure my sister was and if she knew it was day. Did she know she was a prisoner? I was glad the din of musicians and cheers from the crowd prevented Jacob from speaking to me although he looked as though he wanted to. By the time we completed the circuit of Haran, I was, if anything, more nervous. The litter stopped. Laban lifted me out. On his supporting arm I walked into the courtyard of our house. Each step was an act of will and pride. At last I stood beside Jacob. Through the thick veil, I could just make out his face. He smiled and love shown from those brown eyes.

"He doesn't know," I whispered to myself. It was of some comfort.

Abiram, the *gal*, began to pronounce the words that joined us as husband and wife. The ceremony complete, I started to regain some confidence. On Jacob's arm I walked to the dais that was set up for the happy couple. Then the feast began. The food Bilhah, Zilpah, and I had labored over was devoured. I noticed how often and assiduously my father kept Jacob's cup filled with wine. Every good wish for happiness and many children was a reason for Laban to urge another cup on my husband.

Utu, the sun god, slid down the arch of the sky. Darkness crept up but torches were lit so the merriment could continue. My confidence began to ebb away as Inanna rose in the east. When he rose to the top of the sky, I would be taken to the bridal tent. My eyes kept slipping to the tent in the center of the courtyard. A week of seclusion with his bride was the prize every groom received. I had no idea how Jacob would react to the woman he really married. Too soon the bridesmaids led me to the tent opening. Zilpah appeared to attend me.

"I will join you soon, my beloved." Jacob's words sent a shaft of despair to my heart.

"I have this night, at least," I consoled myself as Zilpah removed the bridal finery. She helped me into the soft pile of skins and pillows arranged so lovingly by Rachel for her adored Jacob. I remembered watching her and feeling like a snake as I prepared to steal her groom.

"Blow out the lamp," I whispered the last instruction as Zilpah gathered the garments before leaving the tent.

"Pleasant night, my mistress," she said. I lay alone in the dark that was lit only by the hateful full face of Nanna shining in the sky. The sounds of merriment ebbed and flowed outside amid the flickering torches. First, I heard boisterous voices approaching and then my father's voice.

"You have my prize possession, my boy." To me his voice sounded too hearty. "Be gentle, for she is a shy bride."

"Father Laban," Jacob's words were slightly slurred, "I will honor her with my life."

The tent flap made a rustling sound as Jacob brushed through it. "Are you here, my love?" His voice sounded tentative and his shape moved closer.

"Yes," I whispered. My heart pounded so loudly I was sure he would hear.

"Shall I light a lamp, beloved?" I heard him fumbling for the lamp-stand as his eyes adjusted to the dimness after the glare of the torches.

"No!" Terror made my voice harsh.

"Don't be afraid." By the moon's guiding light, he found the bed, and then his hands found my hands.

"So cold!" He kissed the palm and each fingertip. "Are you afraid of me?"

"Yes ... No ..." How would Rachel answer? My senses were jumping. I heard him pulling off his clothes and then he slid under the blanket next to me. I couldn't stop shaking.

Mistaking my terror of discovery for shyness, my husband gently slid his arm beneath my head. Ever so lovingly, he began to kiss and caress my face and lips. Gradually, my panic was replaced by awe and desire as his loving hands awakened new sensations throughout my body. The brief moment of pain as he made me his was swallowed up in the explosion of joy as I gave myself to his love.

For the rest of the night, I let myself forget the morning. I listened to his words of love and whispered them back to him. My exploring hands learned to delight in the feel of his body. Finally, he slept in my arms, exhausted by our lovemaking. I dozed lightly and awoke when the first light touched the tent. Not wanting the man to awaken, I lay barely breathing and watched him sleep.

"I love you Jacob bar Isaac," I whispered, taking in every detail of his face and hair and body. "Thank you God of my husband for this night." The illusion was nearing an end. He stretched and yawned then rolled toward me.

"My dearest love ..." The words died on his lips when he saw my face, not Rachel's. The shock was quickly followed by fury. Outraged, he demanded, "What have you done? Where is my Rachel?"

I cringed back from the rage in his eyes. Throwing himself out of the bed, he rapidly wrapped his clothing around his body. He threw a tunic at me.

"Put that on," the man snarled. "We will see your father and get to the bottom of this farce."

Amazingly, my hands didn't shake as I dressed. A calm of inevitability settled over me. Jacob grabbed my wrist. He stormed across the yard dragging me behind him.

"Laban, Laban bar Nahor come out and face me!" The furious voice resonated through the house. I was sure he could be heard to the ends of Haran.

Father must have expected such a greeting for he came out fully dressed, with hair and beard neatly oiled and a calm expression on his face. "My son, what is this?"

Jacob spun me forward into my father's arms. "You tricked me!" The words were level and hard. The brown eyes that were usually gentle and loving were glinting with rage.

I felt myself starting to shake and sob. The beautiful, passionate love of the night was a quickly fading mirage.

"I worked for you for seven years to marry Rachel." The man seemed a stranger as he spat the words at Laban.

"You worked seven years to wed my daughter," my father's voice remained calm in the face of the onslaught. "Leah is my eldest daughter."

A sound like a growl came from the young man. Ignoring the interruption, Laban continued, "It is not our custom for the younger to be married before the elder."

"You tricked me." The words were repeated harshly. "What have you done with Rachel?" His inflection softened slightly at her name.

"My son," Laban's appearance of shock was masterful, "I would not harm my own daughter. She is safe."

"I want to see her."

"Complete your week with Leah," the wheedling trader's tone was back, "then you shall not only see Rachel, you may wed her also.

Daring a glance at my husband, I saw surprise, then amazement and hope flashed across his face.

"You would give me Rachel also?"

"There is the small matter of a bride price." Laban's hand moved in a deprecating fashion.

"And …" Jacob prodded. Resignation replaced anger as he saw the plan unfold to snare him.

I, too, was not surprised to hear Laban say with a smile, "Another seven years seems fair." My father had used me to delay the loss of the young man's free labor.

"I *will* wed Rachel in a week?" The intent look was met with a hearty laugh.

"Have I not said so? My son, take your bride."

He lifted me from his chest where I had burrowed my face to hide from the anger of the man I married. I found myself back in Jacob's arms. The man held me loosely.

Laban urged, "Go enjoy your bridal week. In seven days you will be the envy of Haran. A man with two lovely young brides."

Jacob turned and began to walk toward the courtyard. A nudge from my father sent me plodding after him.

"Jacob bar Isaac, this was not Leah's idea." My father's words followed us. I was not sure my husband heard or cared. His back was stiff with injured pride and rage. He didn't even wait for me before letting the flap fall back into place. I lifted it and followed him into the dim and cramped space of the bridal tent. It was not the same. The joy was gone.

Jacob threw himself down on the bed. I stood in front of him unable to meet his eyes. Pride kept me from collapsing at his feet to plead for his understanding and forgiveness, if not his love. The silence stretched out. I dared a look at the man. He was not looking at me. He head was in his hands. Then I knelt.

"Jacob, my husband, I am sorry." When he said nothing, I plunged ahead. "This is my fault. Father could find no other groom and took advantage of you to marry me off. It is true, I prayed for a groom so I would not be shamed at Rachel's marriage. I even prayed to your One God." Once started, I couldn't seem to stop. "My husband, I would have stopped the ceremony if I could. I was sure that you would see that I was not Rachel."

"Under the veil and gown, how was I to know?" At least he responded, if only in a growl.

"I don't know," I sobbed. "I was terrified that you would expose me. I never thought of your feelings when Laban proposed the plan. It is true that I ignored what I knew would be Rachel's despair." Taking a deep breath, I finished in a rush, "Jacob, my husband, I do love you. I will serve you and bear you children. Please do not send me away." Spent with emotion, I sank into a miserable pile at his feet.

There was no reply and my heart died. I could not endure six days of angry or uncaring silence from the man who was my husband. "God of Jacob," my soul cried out, "I am sorry. Help me make it up to Jacob." I looked up at the man, begging for forgiveness.

Silently, he stared at me. I knew too well what he saw. In place of his beloved was an unattractive round face surrounded by tangled strands of straight, dull black hair. Not at all like the wavy auburn hair that framed the delicate face and bright eyes of my sister. It was not the face he wanted to see. Against my will, a single tear rolled down my cheek. I dropped my head to hide the growing despair at his endless silence and stern look.

I had no pride left as I made a final desperate plea, "You loved me last night. I will make you happy."

"Last night you were Rachel." The words were brutal blows.

I could not give up. Boldly, I knelt and pressed against him. "Can Rachel give herself more freely than I did?"

He pushed me away to stand and pace the confined area. My hope dwindled with each angry step he took. I heard him muttering to himself and realized that he was praying.

"God, you are the God who met me at Bethel. You promised to prosper my journey. Is this your punishment for my theft of Esau's blessing … that you take from me my love and give me her sister instead? I took my brother's birthright as this woman has taken away Rachel's dream and my desire."

Jacob paused to lift the tent flap and gaze toward the East, toward the land where the gods live. He stood so still that I barely breathed. My spirit reached out to him and to any god who was listening.

"God of my husband, if you hear, help him. May the gods of my childhood bring him comfort and peace. I only want his happiness."

Finally, he turned back to me and let the tent close behind him. He came toward me. I sat frozen on the bed. The morning light placed his face in the shadow so that I could not see if he was still angry. Standing beside the bed, the man placed his hands on each side of my head and tilted it up.

"Leah, I will not send you away or punish you for this scheme. Before my God, I am not blameless. I took the blessing intended for my brother. The God of my Fathers has shown me that I am forgiven, but that I cannot hold this trick against you."

"My husband." The whisper was full of hope and tentative joy. I pulled myself to my knees and wrapped my arms around his body. My head rested on his heart. I heard it pounding steadily. Bravely, I slipped my hand inside his garment to touch his skin. Ever so gently I ran my fingers across his back until I felt the heartbeat quicken. My one thought was to please him and make him forget the anger.

I succeeded so well that we lay tangled together in the tumbled skins and blankets when Zilpah slipped into the tent with a tray of food. The sun was high and she was apologetic.

Keeping her face averted, she murmured, "The master thought you might want something to eat."

Jacob raised himself on one elbow, "Tell your wily master this," although his lips smiled, the words were cold, "Jacob bar Isaac will keep his bargain. See that Laban bar Nahor keeps his, lest Haran hear of his deceit."

"Yes, lord ... master," she fumbled over the title, confused by the message.

"Exactly as I said it, girl," he warned as she scuttled out of the tent.

I put my hand on his shoulder, "Husband?"

"I will keep your father to the whole deal," he said sitting up and reaching for the food.

So I had not erased Rachel, but I still had the rest of my bridal week to treasure. It was the best week of my life. I stored up memories of the gentle lover, Jacob, as well as the impatient and passionate man that he could be. We talked, and he told me of his mother, my aunt Rebekah. His words painted a picture of the land and tents and flocks he left behind. There was a tinge of homesickness in his voice when he spoke of his father Isaac.

"He is getting old. I pray I can return before he dies."

"You love him." The statement needed no reply.

"Yes, I do." He sounded almost surprised. "I always thought it was my mother I loved most. My father preferred Esau because he is adventurous. He loves to hunt and travel far. I preferred learning to tend the sheep and the fields."

After a minute, he laughed softly, "Look at which of us is miles away from Canaan. I am here while Esau remains safely at home." He shook his head and laughed again before soberly continuing. "I fled for my life. Will I ever be able to return?"

More to comfort him than from any real conviction, I replied, "I am sure that the God you worship will bring you back to Canaan and your father. Hasn't he promised you that?"

"True," he pondered briefly, "but I have seven more years of service to your father."

I had to lower my eyes because a flash of jealousy rushed through me. He still, even after a week, yearned for Rachel. "Let's think of happy things on this our last night. Think of our sons," I urged drawing him into my arms where I, at least, forgot about my sister for awhile.

# Chapter 4

It was hard to leave the security of the bridal tent, harder still to face the look of triumph in Rachel's eyes as she raced into Jacob's open arms.

Her words twisted the knife of guilt in my soul. "My Jacob, at last we shall be together."

His lips buried themselves in her curls and I ceased to exist.

Laban looked on benignly, content that his daughters were safely wed and that he had arranged for seven more years of free labor from his young relative. Even my brothers were smiling smugly as they watched the reunion. No one had a thought for me.

"Come children, there is plenty of time for that." My father's hand on Jacob's shoulder caused him to raise his head.

Zilpah tugged my hand and I allowed her to lead me away to finish preparations for Rachel's wedding.

"Bilhah is to be Rachel's maid," the girl told me in an attempt at conversation.

"I made him happy, but all along it was Rachel in his heart." My head bowed I whispered the truth to myself. I barely heard the maid. "Why could he not see that I have love to give, too?"

"Mistress." I looked up to see Zilpah holding out the bowl of water for washing. The sympathy in her eyes nearly made me cry.

"You will bear him many sons," she said encouragingly. Listlessly, I took the cloth from her and dried my hands.

"I pray to the God of my husband that is so." My unspoken hope was that the man would love me when he saw that I bore healthy sons.

The day of Rachel's wedding passed in a blur. I tried to ignore the whispers from the women.

"Probably couldn't wait to marry Leah off when a willing kinsman was found."

"Poor Rachel had to wait."

"Isn't Jacob really the son of Laban's sister? Did you hear that she was barren for many years and then finally had twin sons?"

"I remember when that servant came and Rebekah went off to Canaan to marry the son of Abraham the Wanderer."

There were comments and laughter from the men when Rachel appeared unveiled.

"Not taking any chances this time, is he?"

"Must have been a shock to wake up next to Leah."

They hurriedly changed the subject when they saw me. The damage was done. My old friend, jealousy, was back. I lowered my head so no one would see the pain burning in my eyes.

"Rachel, Rachel. It is all anyone thinks about." I let myself wallow in self-pity throughout my sister's bridal week. Outwardly, I went about my daily duties of drawing water, baking, and cleaning. Zilpah faithfully stayed at my side as I divided my time between Laban's house and my new home. Bilhah busied herself preparing Rachel's belongings in the adjacent house provided for Jacob and his family.

One day I wandered through my father's house looking at all the familiar things. Everything reminded me of some event. I remembered Rachel's birth and later my mother's death. My first attempt at weaving was found rolled up in a corner. With tears rolling down my cheeks, I looked at the crooked warp and tried to recall the ten-year old who sat near her mother. My gentle mother's words and instructions from her bed came back to me.

"Leah, my dear child, I won't be here to teach you all that I dreamed of. I pray the gods keep watch over you to keep the beauty in your eyes and heart. Come, show me your weaving. Look at the beautiful colors you have chosen. This is what I see in you, my sweet Leah, colors and a loving heart."

Carefully I tucked the scrap into a corner of the leather box that held a few other mementos. Then I closed the lid to shut out the past. After a last look around the room that had been mine, I picked up the box to carry it to my new home.

For fourteen years, I had been in charge of Laban's household. Now, I would share the housekeeping duties with Rachel in a new home. I knew that she didn't like to cook and clean and weave; but, for Jacob, she would do anything. At least Zilpah and Bilhah were also coming. They would help with the chores when Rachel was with the sheep.

Rachel's wedding week ended too soon and we were all together in our new home. As I had foreseen, she continued to go with Jacob to the fields with the sheep. I spent my days in a fever of cleaning and baking and weaving. Jacob would have no cause to find fault with my housekeeping, but I doubted that he noticed. Sometimes I heard the whispers of the lovers, but usually I dropped into an exhausted, dreamless sleep as soon as I lay down.

The full moon came again, reminding me that only a month ago I was a bride. Staring at the rising orb, I sighed, "Inanna, what good is it to have a husband who does not love or come to me?" I followed it with a prayer to Jacob's God. "If you are the One God, let me have a sign to give me hope." Nothing happened and I turned away to finish the evening chores.

I heard Rachel giggle as I plodded to my bed. She rarely spoke to me now. Her days were spent in the fields and her nights in Jacob's arms. So, when she sought me out a few days later, I was surprised.

"Leah, I cannot go with Jacob today," she whispered, catching my arm as I lifted the jar to go to the well. "My monthly flow has come. I must stay in my room. Why are women so cursed?"

I started to reply, but a sudden thought stopped me. My monthly flow had not come. Rapidly I calculated. Indeed I should have needed the rags soon after Rachel's bridal week. Now it was over a moon cycle since my wedding.

"Could it be?" I pressed my hands to my belly with a wild hope racing through my heart. "A baby, a son! Might not Jacob then see me as desirable?"

Keeping my thoughts to myself, I assured Rachel that I would tell Jacob why she was not coming with him. I came upon him as he prepared to open the pen and herd the flocks out.

"Rachel cannot come today," I blurted out, color rushing to my face when he looked at me. "Her monthly time has come and she must stay inside."

"I see," was all he said.

Watching him stride away, I promised myself that I would be held in his arms this night. I spent the day preparing a special meal that I took to him myself after dismissing Zilpah and Bilhah. My secret hope made me bold. I looked at my husband with all the love that was in my heart.

"You look as though you have a secret," he teased. "Tell me what it is."

As much as I wanted to tell him, I had to wait until I was sure. So I only stroked his hair and told him, "My husband, the secret is I love you."

He laughed and pulled me down onto his lap to caress my cheek. "The secret is, my wife, that you want me to make love to you."

Surprised, but not unwilling, I relaxed in his arms. I ignored the whisper in my mind: "He is only kissing you because Rachel isn't here." Sternly, I ordered that voice into silence. Jacob held me and not my sister. Joyfully I gave myself to him. The hope in my heart made me wild with desire.

Jacob's words tempted me as he gently kissed the top of my head while I lay in his arms, happy after his lovemaking.

"My wife, the Lord God of my Father Isaac has given me a jewel in your devotion," he mused. "Despite all, you offer yourself to me freely. What further blessing can I hope for but a son?"

Even as I opened my mouth to speak, he kissed my forehead and rolled on his side. Snores told me he was soon asleep. I lay awake in prayer: "Lord God of my husband, let me be the one to give him the further blessing he desires." Finally, I slept close to his back. I was content for the moment and forced myself to forget his love for Rachel.

It was Rachel, in her seclusion, who became suspicious. She came to me in the kitchen. "You haven't had your monthly flow, have you?" Her dark eyes were accusing.

"No, I realized that yesterday," I acknowledged.

"Are you ... do you think?" She was quite excited.

"I might be," I hedged. "In a couple of weeks I'll be sure."

My sister's joy was surprising. "Leah, I think that would be wonderful! How happy Jacob would be!" Joyfully she hugged me. I was ashamed to think that I would not have rejoiced for her.

"You must not tell him until I am sure," I cautioned and she promised.

"Of course you must be the one to tell our husband. You should tell him now."

"No," I insisted, firmly resisting the idea just as I had the night before in Jacob's arms.

Rachel returned to the fields after a week. I remonstrated with her but she remained firm. "Jacob is working to earn me," she pointed out, "I should be helping him now more than ever."

I let her go. Bilhah and Zilpah fell into their old roles as my helpers. Each day I became more certain that I was pregnant. First Bilhah and then Zilpah realized the truth when they saw me caressing my belly. Their excitement made me smile.

"I will tell Jacob soon." The promise was made to myself as well as the maids.

There never seemed to be a good time to tell my husband. I wanted to be alone with him, but Rachel was always at his side. At last, I could stand the secret no longer. I knelt before Jacob after he finished eating. "My husband, I would speak to you."

He tilted his head and with a raised eyebrow replied, "You don't have to ask my permission."

I looked at Rachel, who giggled, "I know ..." then she clapped her hand over her mouth.

Jacob looked curiously from one wife to the other. I scowled at my sister who continued to shake her head and giggle.

This wasn't the way I wanted it to be. It was not how I imagined my announcement. I started to get up. He leaned forward to place his hands on my shoulders.

"No, Leah," the gentle use of my name made me look at the man, "tell me what you want." He frowned slightly at Rachel who sat back with sparkling eyes but the giggles stopped.

"I ... that is ... my husband ... we, you..." Tongue-tied, I couldn't get the words out.

"I'll tell," Rachel offered.

Darting an angry look at her, I looked into Jacob's eyes. They were curious and a little worried. With a deep breath I blurted out the words, "I am with child."

Astonishment and then joy appeared on his face. With a broad smile, he jumped to his feet and swung me off the ground into an ecstatic embrace. I heard Rachel laughing in the background, but my focus was on his words. "My wife! Leah, I am the happiest of men! You will give me a son! The first of many!"

I was dizzy with joy when he set me down. Rachel kissed me on the cheek and slyly whispered, "I told you he would be happy."

Being the focus of everyone's attention was uncomfortable. I was relieved when after a few days Jacob quit announcing the event to everyone he met. Life settled back into the normal routine. My sister and my husband spent the days in the fields, always returning for the evening meal. The warm summer weather meant that Jacob spent most nights sleeping with the flocks so they could graze all night and grow fat. I, too, grew plump as summer turned to fall and the harvest was brought in.

Rachel was excited about the coming birth. When she was with Jacob and the sheep, she worked on little clothes for the baby. She used the rest of the fine linen Laban bought for her wedding robe. "The firstborn son deserves a fine swaddling gown," she informed me when I protested that she should keep the material for her own use.

I was content and barely jealous of the time Jacob spent with Rachel. His obvious joy in my pregnancy was enough. He liked to rest his head on my blossoming belly during the fall evenings after the sheep were penned in and the meal eaten.

"My Leah," he said with his hand on mine, "you are giving me a great gift. The God of my Father is gracious."

The days grew shorter and shorter. Preparations for the yearly fire rekindling were made. The chief temple priestess and the *Gal* performed the ritual consummation on the roof of the temple. I remembered stories told by my grandfather, Nahor. He detailed the grand celebrations when the King and the Great Priestess of the Ziggurat of Ur called back Dimuzi from the Ningizzida, Land of No Return, to renew the world by the yearly marriage with Inanna.

Jacob had always distanced himself from the feast saying merely, "Abraham, my grandfather, left the gods of Ur and Haran to follow the One God. I can do no less."

The simple statement always affected me deeply. That the man would calmly stand against the entire community on this most important day of the year called to my soul. This year, with his child growing in me, I refused to attend the observance.

"Jacob's absence has not caused the seasons to stop," I pointed out when Rachel and Laban confronted me angrily. "I carry his child. His son will learn to worship the God of his father."

Jacob placed his hand on my shoulder in affirmation. "It is well that Leah stays away from the crowds. You may go and worship as you desire. My wife has chosen to stay home this year."

"I think you are a fool to flout Inanna," Rachel hissed. "How can you expect love and many children if you do?"

I stayed silent thinking that it was not the goddess Inanna who had given me my husband or child, but the One God that Abraham the Wanderer followed.

"We will make your excuses." My father strode off beside my sister. I knew they were both worried, as well as angry. My own heart was pounding in a mixture of fear and confidence.

"My Leah," Jacob's voice held a note of deep respect, "that was bravely done. May the God of my Fathers bless you for your courage so that you may bear many sons." He smiled at me and I was suddenly unafraid.

Except for more whispers and stares, no one in Haran mentioned my odd behavior. However, I did hear some crones attributing my conduct to the nearness of the baby's birth. Preparations for the child were complete. The blankets and swaddling cloths were ready. I was slow and clumsy in my movements and often my back ached. Late one afternoon, I stood staring at the cold, cloudy landscape slowly rubbing my hand across my lower back. Snow had dusted the higher hills and a chill breeze blew through the valley.

"Rachel and Jacob will be in from the fields anytime," I mentioned to Zilpah.

"Yes," she responded, "Utu makes a short journey today."

"He is hidden behind the clouds," I remarked. A sudden spasm of pain caught me by surprise. I gasped and gripped the doorpost.

"Mistress Leah!" The faithful girl hurried to my side.

"It is nothing, let's finish the meal." I turned to walk across the floor. Another spasm stuck.

I caught Zilpah's arm in such a grip that she cried out. The pain proceeded to attack again when I reached for the platter of bread.

"Zilpah," I gasped in clarity, "I think it is time."

Immediately, she was at my side. On her arm, I managed to get to my room before another pain struck.

"I'll send Bilhah for the midwife," she told me. I could only nod as another contraction gripped my body.

She left the room. I heard rapid voices and then Bilhah's running feet. Zilpah returned to my side and attempted to make me comfortable. It seemed hours later when the midwife returned with Bilhah and not a moment too soon. A quick look told her that the baby was indeed ready to be born. Supported by Zilpah's strong arms, I squatted to deliver the child.

"Push with the next pain," the midwife's orders were brief. "Again!" Then, "Gently, now, here he is."

A healthy cry was music to my ears. I leaned back against Zilpah.

"You have a fine, healthy son!" The midwife's words completed my joy. The tiny bundle was wrapped and pressed into my arms. Looking down at the little red face, I felt such a wave of love spread across my body that I started to cry.

"You must give him suck," instructed the woman. She helped me place my son at my breast. In a moment, he was happily nursing. Vaguely, I heard Rachel enter the room.

She knelt beside me, "Sister, we have a son!"

"Jacob?" I looked up to ask.

"He is outside," she giggled. "The man is afraid to come into the house."

"As it should be," nodded the midwife with a smile of her own as she admired her handiwork.

Tired, but eager to see my husband, I urged Rachel, "Tell him to come in."

The midwife intervened, "After you are settled, then your husband may come in."

Between them all, I was enthroned in the bed with pillows behind my head and blankets to cover both my son and me.

When she was satisfied, the midwife ushered the women out.

"You may come in now," she announced like a queen bestowing an honor. "May your son grow to be a blessing."

She held the curtain aside for Jacob as she left. Tentatively and almost shyly, he entered the room.

"Come, my husband, see our son." I held out my hand in encouragement.

He knelt beside the bed. I was surprised to feel him stroking my hair with one hand.

"Leah, a son!" He seemed utterly amazed. The adoration in his eyes brought tears to mine.

I held out the tiny bundle. With an almost fearful finger, he touched one cheek.

"May we name him Reuben?" I asked. "He is our son and his name should proclaim that to the world."

"Whatever you want," he replied. In awe, he continued to stroke his son's head with one finger.

My heart rang with praise. "Surely, God of my husband, this is how you take away my disgrace among the women. You have given me a son, and now Jacob will love me."

I was wrong. Too soon he called for Rachel. With his arm around her waist, he announced, "I have a son! His name is Reuben! Come, let us tell your father."

I was left alone with my baby. Once again I was the outsider, even within the family. Then I looked at my son sleeping in my arms. I had born Jacob a son while Rachel remained barren.

Laban and my brothers hurried to offer congratulations, but stayed only long enough to admire the fine boy in my arms.

After everyone left, I lay looking at my sleeping son. "Reuben, my son," I crooned softly, "you are the firstborn of Jacob bar Isaac. No one can take that right from you. Rachel may hold Jacob's heart, but I hold you, my son. You are the heir. No one can take that from you!" I repeated the promise to my child, holding him close to my heart.

# Chapter 5

Reuben seemed to grow bigger each day. After the required days of isolation, I returned to my normal life. My son played on a soft pile of goatskins while I worked in the kitchen or swept the dirt floors. Bilhah and Zilpah loved to play with him. Often I had to remind them that there was still work to be done.

"I am so glad you are back," Rachel sighed. "It is impossible to get everything done."

With a big sister hug, I told her, "It just takes practice."

"Well, I'm glad you are here and I can return to the sheep," she told me with an answering hug.

Jacob overcame his fear of the tiny boy and began to play with his son in the evenings.

"Look at him holding my finger so tightly!" He exclaimed. "You are going to be a strong man, my son!" He picked up the baby and after they stared at each other, Reuben tangled his fingers in his father's beard.

"Envious of my whiskers already, are you?" My husband laughed.

Content to see them happy together, I leaned against the doorframe and watched.

Spring came with the busy lambing time. I rarely saw Rachel and Jacob, for they spent all their time in the fields. But, I was not lonely, for I had Reuben to love.

One night after the lambs were all delivered, Jacob took my hand as I stood watching Reuben sleep. His kiss on my neck caused my knees to shake.

"Come to me," he said, his lips seeking mine. Surprised but willing, I allowed him to lead me off to the bed. I had forgotten how sweet his caresses were. Without reservation, I gave myself to my husband. In his arms I could believe that he did indeed love me.

The week that followed was bliss that I stored up in my memory. Rachel in her monthly time remained in her room. I could pretend that ours was a simple family and no jealousy marred my thoughts. Too soon, though, Rachel rejoined the evening gatherings. I was not surprised when she accompanied Jacob to bed. The glow of his attention upheld me for several days. I got used to the routine of having my husband for a week each month. Even when I suspected that I was again pregnant, I hid the fact in order to enjoy his love.

Too soon the reality became obvious, even to Jacob. "My wife," he asked as he stroked my body one night in the early fall, "are you keeping something from me?"

Trying to pretend innocence, I hedged, "Why?"

His hand rested on my rounding belly and his eyes looked into mine. "Are you going to have another child?" The question hung in the air.

Finally, I nodded, "Yes, my husband."

He rolled away from me and I felt cold.

"Aren't you glad?" My voice was thin.

"Of course." He turned to look at me and saw the tears standing in my eyes. "Leah, you know I cannot lay with you now."

"That's foolish," I stated, sitting up. "You have not stopped for the past three months."

"I'm sorry," he looked unhappy, "now I know and I cannot …" Jacob turned away to shrug into his clothes.

"Would it be different if I was Rachel?" The words slipped out before I thought.

Slowly the man turned to look at me. His brows drew into a frown. "That is unfair. It would not matter. It is not right for a man to bed with a pregnant woman."

"I'm sorry." My hand reached for him. "I just …"

He interrupted me, "There is no more to be said." At the door he paused to ask, "When is the child to be born?"

"Probably a moon turning after the Day of No Moon at the New Year."

I knew he was angry at my deceit, but I could not be too sorry. The extra months of his love were stored in my heart. However, now Jacob refused to speak to me.

I cried to God, "Was it so wrong to seek my husband's love against the laws of man?"

"You have mocked the gods," Rachel warned. "The child will not be healthy."

Now that the secret was out, I could accept congratulations from everyone. I overheard talk at the well that made me smile to myself.

"Here comes Leah. She is pregnant again."

"She looks almost pretty when she is expecting."

"True, she's one of the lucky ones who can look glowing even when bulging with child."

"You know, I think she likes to be pregnant."

The last statement was true. Each pregnancy proved that I was better than Rachel. I felt fulfilled and alive when carrying a child. And, I hoped that Jacob would grow to love me.

The days became shorter, and each evening we all gathered together to play with Reuben. I rejoiced in my son as he tried to stand and smiled happily when he learned to toddle to his father. With winter, came the New Year. One morning I sent Zilpah for the midwife. Before noon I held Simeon in my arms. Despite Rachel's concerns, he was healthy and vocal.

"God of my husband, you saw I was hated for my desire. You have given me this strong son. Surely your blessing is on me, for the child was conceived in love."

Jacob and Rachel hurried in from the fields.

"See," I told Jacob, "no harm. A fine, healthy son has come from our union."

Staring at the tiny face scrunched in a cry, Jacob smiled. I relaxed, for the smile included me.

"Truly, the God of my Fathers is gracious. My Leah has delivered a healthy son." He sealed his forgiveness with a kiss.

Rachel, too, gave me a quick hug, but I saw sorrow in her eyes as she looked at Jacob.

"You will also have a son one day," I told her several months later when I found her crying.

"Do not speak to me of such things!" she stormed. "You are pregnant again! Surely the gods mock me!"

"The God of Jacob has been good to me and made me fruitful," I replied with a note of pride that I could not suppress.

"Jacob loves me!" she hissed. "I, too, must have children. My sons will be stronger and wiser than yours."

A few days later I heard loud voices from the sheep pen. "You spend all your time with Leah and her sons!" Rachel was uncharacteristically raging.

"My love," Jacob sought to placate her, "we spend each day together. You share my bed at night."

"Give me sons!" My sister was practically screaming.

"Rachel, have I ever withheld my love from you?" There was a hint of exasperation in his voice.

"Then it is your God," she accused. "Ask this wonderful God of yours to give me sons."

"I have prayed," he told her with a sigh. "Have you asked God yourself?"

"My offerings and petitions have been given to every god I can think of," the shrill voice replied. "You don't know what it is like to endure the smug smiles of the village girls. They look at me and think I am rejected, especially the younger ones with their children. Still I am childless."

"Wife, the blame does not lie with me!" For the first time, Jacob was angry with my sister. "Ask the God of my Fathers why you have no sons—not me!" I heard his rapid footsteps approaching.

A wailing cry, "Jacob!" trailed after him.

I tried to comfort my sister when she came in, but she pushed me away. "You don't understand, you with your sons. The gods have closed my womb. Now Jacob hates me."

"Our husband will not stay angry," I told her. In my heart I knew that his love for this woman would overcome any brief anger. "Ask the God of Jacob for children," I counseled. She simply turned her back.

"Leave me alone. Take care of your sons. Leave me to my childlessness."

Rachel stayed in her room all the next day. Jacob trudged off to the fields with the sheep without her company. I knew he was saddened by Rachel's silence. Late in the afternoon, I heard her call Bilhah.

Jacob relaxed after finishing his meal. The boys played on and around him. I allowed myself to relax and leaned back on the pillows to rest my back from the weight of my bulging belly. The baby kicked, and I smiled to see the movement through my clothes.

The peaceful scene was interrupted by Rachel's entrance. She was towing Bilhah. The maid wore one of Rachel's gowns. Her hair was smoothly combed and adorned with one of Rachel's scarves.

Even before she spoke, I understood. "My husband, forgive my outburst," Rachel knelt before Jacob. She ignored the babies and me, looking only at her husband.

I saw his eyes soften. She continued before he could speak. "My love, take my maid Bilhah in my place. Let her bear children for me. The gods have closed my womb, but I pray they will make Bilhah fruitful."

"Rachel." Jacob sat up to reach for her hand.

Keeping her head bent, my sister placed Bilhah's fingers in the hand of her love. A lump came into my throat. I barely understood the depth of despair that drove her to this action.

"Rachel, my love." Jacob tried to make her look at him. She avoided his hand and scrambled to her feet.

"Bilhah will bear my children, my husband. I give her to you." She hurried from the room. I saw the hint of tears sparkling in her eyes as she rushed past.

Jacob sat stunned staring alternately at me and at Bilhah.

"It is a gift from the depths of her love," I told him. "Come boys, it is time to tell Papa goodnight."

Reuben toddled over to his father and Simeon crawled after him like the shadow of his big brother. I tucked them into their pallet absentmindedly. I was thinking of Rachel and her gift to Jacob.

Bilhah did conceive and Rachel put on a joyful face. Soon it was time for me to be delivered of my third son. I named him Levi, telling myself, "Surely Jacob will turn to me for I have three healthy sons."

Still he clung to his love for my sister. He spent the evenings playing with my three sons even though he spent his days in the fields with Rachel and his nights with her in his arms.

"Look at Reuben," he gloated as his oldest son took up the shepherd's staff. Although it towered above him, the boy assumed a watchful stance while Simeon and Levi crawled around him.

"They are my sheep," the boy told his father who roared with laughter.

Simeon tired of the game and toddled over to attempt to wrest the staff from his brother. Jacob's swift action saved the waving staff from breaking the water jar in the corner. I scooped Levi from the floor and out of the ensuing wrestling match between father and sons. Watching them, I realized that for the first time in my life I was content. Jacob did not adore me as he did Rachel, but he cared for me and loved our sons.

"God of my husband," I breathed a prayer of thanksgiving, "you have given me full measure of joy despite my sister. The child in my womb will be named Judah, for I praise the Lord God of Jacob."

The fact that I was pregnant again was something I had not yet shared with anyone, for Bilhah's time was near. Indeed, the next day Zilpah ran for the midwife. Rachel held the maid in her arms, and while encouraging her, she seemed almost to be laboring too, for she was panting and sweating by the time the baby was born.

"A son for the house of Jacob," the midwife announced.

"His name is Dan," Rachel whispered, "for the gods judged me innocent and gave me a son."

I heard the vindication in her voice and she shot me a proud look.

Jacob was ecstatic. "I am most blessed by the God of Abraham and Isaac. He has indeed judged me faithful."

When my fourth son was born he agreed that it was time to praise the Lord and we named the vigorous baby with the mop of black hair, Judah.

Still Rachel bore no children. Again she approached Jacob. "My husband, let Bilhah bear me another son."

He shook his head, but she insisted. A boiling shot of jealousy sent scalding tears to my eyes as I stood just outside the door. I had hoped that he would come to me for Rachel's time was upon her.

Jacob's words did nothing to ease the pain. "Very well, my love," I heard the surrender in his voice. "If it is your wish, I shall go to Bilhah, but I would rather it was you."

I fled to my room where the tears were buried in a pillow. Gradually, hard determination cleared my head. My husband had not visited my bed since Judah's birth.

"God of my husband," I swore, "I, too, will give my maid to Jacob. Grant that she may be fruitful and bear your handmaid and your servant a strong son."

Surprisingly, I found Jacob alone the next night. Zilpah had agreed to my plan only after much pleading and a snapped order. "You are my maid to do with as I choose. For my husband, you will bear a son."

Now I faced the man. Fear of his response nearly made me change my mind. His words hardened my resolve.

"Leah, how comfortable it is to come home to a meal and neat home. Your sister is my beloved wife, but her skills lie with the flocks, not with the home."

I swallowed hard against the choking envy as I knelt as his feet. Keeping my eyes downcast so he wouldn't see the jealousy that prompted my action, I spoke. "My lord husband, from my heart I give you my maid Zilpah. The Lord your God seeks to bless you with many sons. Take Zilpah as you have Bilhah and bear sons with her." The carefully rehearsed words hung in the air.

Jacob stared at me. I knew it without looking up. "Why, my wife?" he asked. "You have born sons for me."

"I have ceased bearing," I replied, holding back words of recrimination and hurt. "Therefore, I beg you bear sons with

Zilpah. My lord husband, accept this gift from me." I barely breathed for he continued to study me.

Finally, he spoke. "If this will make you content, then I shall go to Zilpah." He bent forward to take my face between his hands. "I do not understand you, my wife."

The kiss he pressed on my forehead left me trembling. I wanted to call him back, but it was too late. His rumbling voice was answered by Zilpah's soft one as they left the room. Then silence. Eventually, I forced myself to seek my room. For a long time I lay staring into the darkness wishing that Jacob had refused Zilpah and taken me to his bed. So, it was that I entered the competition for my husband's affection.

The maids' sons were born within a week of each other. I heard Rachel tell Bilhah, "My son will be named Napthali, for I have wrestled with my sister and won. She, too, has had to resort to her maid to give Jacob sons."

The hard lump of anger in my heart took on another layer. I held Zilpah during her labor and when Jacob came to see his son I suggested, "Let us call him Gad. Your God has given you good fortune in the birth of another son."

"Let it be as you say, Leah, for God has indeed given me good fortune. I have seven sons, two wives, and honor in this place. Three more years and my time of service will be at an end."

A year later Asher was born to Zilpah. I held her as she labored, but my heart screamed out at the injustice. For Jacob had gone to her and not to me. I was not surprised, for I was exhausted at the end of every day while Zilpah seemed fresh and cheerful.

"Let us call him Asher," I said, knowing that I lied even as I named him. Happiness was far from my mind.

Jacob's joy and pride only made the jealous thorn dig deeper. My one consolation was of Rachel's barely concealed despair over her own childlessness.

"Why won't the gods hear my cries?" she wailed. "Every day I stop at the shrine and make an offering to Inanna for fertility. Still I remain barren."

"Jacob's love for you doesn't need child to strengthen it." The words sounded hollow even to me.

"No, my sister, a child would complete our relationship."

"He goes to you each night. You are his beloved." The jealousy in my voice hung in the air.

Rachel looked at me curiously. "You have born him four sons. Why would you want more? Why would Jacob come to you?"

Afraid that I would strike her, I turned away. I threw back over my shoulder words filled with venom. "You need not fear losing Jacob's love."

As I rushed off down the street, Rachel's words twisted in my heart. "You never had Jacob's love." I reached the hillside and cried out in anguish. "Why am I so despised? True, I married the man by trickery, but I have sought his love by bearing him sons. Now, even that hope is taken away for Jacob only seeks Rachel's arms."

My thoughts raced in circles as I wept in despair. Eventually, spent from tears, I sent up a whispered prayer. "God of my husband, let me be loved." I sat for a long time in the gathering dusk, feeling something like peace return. Somehow, in that time, I knew I was not alone. I knew that Jacob's God was real and I was comforted.

It was only a few days later when my prayer seemed to be answered. "Mother, see what I have brought you." Reuben handed me a bundle of roots.

Accustomed to their treasured offerings of weeds and rocks, I took the gift. "My son, how thoughtful," I said before glancing at what I held. When I looked closely, my heart started pounding. It was mandrake, for fertility. I looked at Reuben, wondering if he knew the significance of his gift.

"So Father will love you." His innocent words answered my unasked question.

Speechless, I could only stare from the thick roots to my oldest son. Kneeling, I drew him close and kissed the top of his head. Tears rolled down my cheeks. He squirmed away from my emotion.

"I have to go back, Simeon is alone with the sheep."

He ran away before I could say anything. I was still watching the puffs of dust from his running feet when Rachel appeared.

"Mandrake!" her exclamation startled me. "Where did you get it?" she demanded, her eyes greedy.

"Reuben brought it to me. You know how boys bring gifts to their mothers." My thoughtless words made her flinch. Still she pressed on.

"Give it to me," she begged. Her tone took on the wheedling sound my father used when bargaining. "Surely you have more than you need. Spare some for me, my sister, that I may know the joy of a son."

An idea formed in my mind. I bent my head to hide the gleam of hope in my eyes. "Why should I give you my mandrake? Jacob already spends every night with you. What would I gain from giving you this root?" In my hand I held the desired prize, weighing it in my palm. Rachel lifted her hand to take it. I tightened my fist around it. Turning away, I felt her hand on my shoulder.

"Wait."

I stopped but didn't face her.

Her words were forced past gritted teeth. "Sister, my husband may sleep with you tonight for the mandrake."

"He is my husband for a fortnight," I countered.

"No, only a week," she responded after a long stretch of silence. "Else the mandrake will be spoiled."

Then I swung around to look my sister full in the face. I held the root between us. "For this mandrake root, I will have Jacob's love for a week?"

"Yes, Leah, I have agreed." She reached for the root.

"Swear it," I insisted, drawing back.

"Don't you trust me?" she asked with a lift of her chin.

When I didn't respond, she sighed, "Very well, I swear that I will not seek out Jacob for a week. I will leave the house. He will be yours." She grabbed the plant and held it to her breast. "Much good he will do you without this," she muttered triumphantly.

"The God of my husband will be gracious," I replied, trying to convince myself.

To say Jacob was surprised to find me, not Rachel, waiting that night is an understatement. Rachel and the boys were nowhere to be seen. True to her word, she had taken them to visit Laban.

His eyes looked around, searching. "Rachel will not be joining us tonight," I informed him softly. "For the mandrake root that Reuben found, I have bought you for a week."

The man looked affronted for a minute, but then the humor of the situation touched him. He chuckled, "Then I am a prize to be traded?"

"You are my well beloved husband," I countered, kneeling at his side. My hand reached out, almost of its own accord, to touch his arm. It had been so long since Jacob had been with me that I felt almost as nervous as a bride.

"Leah." The name was pronounced slowly.

He looked at me for what seemed like a long time. As always, I wished my hair were thick and wavy like Rachel's. I knew a few strands of gray were creeping into my straight hair. My face bore the lines formed by squinting to see my

husband and sons returning from the fields. It was not
smooth like my sister. Under my tunic, I knew my body was
not as firm as Rachel's. Reminding myself that I had borne
four sons, I tried not to think about my body when Jacob
drew the clothing down off my shoulders. Love and desire
melded into one when he kissed me. As always, my body
responded to his touch and I lost myself in the sensation of
his lovemaking. The week passed too quickly. Each day
dragged by with the humdrum daily tasks. Nights were filled
with the ecstasy of being in my husband's arms.

Rachel, too, was counting the days and wore her most
beguiling gown on the seventh day. I comforted myself by
playing with the children and remembering the week just past.
Before long, I had a new joy to add to my peace of mind. I
was pregnant again! Rachel's grief knew no bounds.
Insulated in the serenity of my pregnancy, I was unaffected
by her tears. She ranted and sobbed in Jacob's arms until he
started finding excuses to stay in the fields with Laban's
animals.

A strong, lusty boy was born. His first cry was heard
throughout the house. I named him Issachar, for as I told
Jacob, "God has given a reward to us." To myself I added, "I
am rewarded for giving Zilpah to my husband."

After Issachar was born, I spent many evenings asking
Jacob about his God. He told me about the One God who
led Abraham from Ur to Haran and then further. My
husband told me how Sarah was barren and Rebekah too,
until God opened their wombs to bear sons. He explained
that God's promise of a homeland and 'descendants of the
stars' was renewed with each generation.

Rachel pouted, uninterested in the discussions of Jacob's
God. I found the stories fascinating and never tired of
hearing of my husband's encounter with the ladder to heaven.

"It was taller than a ziggurat," he said, so I could envision the size, "and angels went up and down the ladder."

"What are angels like?" I wondered, caressing the check of my suckling son.

Jacob stared off across the room, remembering his dream of so many years ago. Rachel leaned forward with interest.

"They are not so much figures, but light," he said as he fumbled for words. "I don't think I can really describe what they are like."

"Your God spoke to you?" I knew the answer, but never ceased to be amazed by the fact that my husband's God actually spoke to him.

As always, his face changed. He looked younger and more relaxed as he recounted the promise. "God said, 'Do not be afraid Jacob, I will be with you and bless you. I will bring you back to your homeland.' "

Realizing I was holding my breath during the recitation, I inhaled. "How mightily your God has fulfilled that promise," I remarked, looking around at his nine sons playing with each other.

With jealousy in her words, Rachel asked, "Then why has your God withheld children from my arms?"

Looking at my sister, Jacob said, "Perhaps God is only waiting to open your womb as with Sarah and Rebekah."

"I don't want to be an old woman when I have a son," she said, stamping her foot angrily as she turned to go.

"Rachel," my words surprised me, "maybe the One God is waiting for you to ask Him alone. Our husband's God is greater than the gods of stone. Turn to Him, sister."

Astonishment on her face was matched by the surprise I saw in Jacob's eyes. "You would turn your back on Inanna and Imdugud?" she gasped.

"The God of Jacob has blessed me," I answered simply and from my heart.

"With sons to make up for the lack of Jacob's love." She spoke softly and venomously close to my ear. Spinning on her heal, she left the room.

I felt my face flush red. Then as my sister disappeared through the doorway, I sank back, drained of confidence. Jacob could not have heard her words. I felt his hand cover mine where it lay limply on the cushion.

"Leah, you make my heart glad." His tone made me open my eyes. "That you believe in the God of my fathers is blessing indeed." My husband bent over me. I could almost trust it was love I saw in his eyes. Then he kissed me. That night in his arms was nearly as magically wonderful as the wedding night when he thought I was Rachel. I was not surprised when I conceived.

Zilpah was appalled. "It is too soon! Issachar is not yet weaned."

Rachel was livid. I heard her angrily accusing Jacob of hating her. "You withhold sons from me and give them to my sister! You claim to love me, but I have nothing to show for it! Give me sons!"

"Am I God?" Jacob's answer was angry. "Can I open what God has closed?"

I heard her wail, "You hate me, for I cannot bear you sons."

"No, my Rachel, my love, I can never hate you. Surely, if we ask the One God together, he will grant you the desire of your heart."

It was not yet to be. Zebulon, son of my honor, was born. My father was as proud as Jacob. Again and again he proclaimed, "My boy, you are indeed blessed of the gods. Look at what you have done for me. My flocks have multiplied under your care, and your family has grown. You are becoming a powerful man in Haran. Truly your son's name, Zebulon, proclaims to all that you are honored by men and by the gods."

I wished that I could erase the sullen look from Rachel's face and have even prayed for her. "God of my husband, You are a generous God showing faithfulness to your servant and to me, his handmaid. Visit Rachel, who has the love of my husband, and grant her a son." Little did I know how the answer to that prayer would change my life.

# Chapter 6

Rachel came to me one day. "Sister, how have you known that you are pregnant?" she asked. Her eager face and white knuckled grip on my arm alerted me to her news.

"Each has been a little different," I replied. "Have you missed the monthly flow?"

She nodded and added, "Two months now and I feel sick all the time. The smell of meat especially makes me ill."

Joyfully, I hugged her. "The God of Jacob has answered our prayers!"

"Then you think I am?" Hopeful brown eyes looked into mine.

"If it is as you say," I nodded, "then you will indeed bear a child for Jacob.

"Let it be a son." She breathed the words like a prayer.

Jacob was jubilant. He was so proud that I overheard a trader new to Haran ask if this was his first child. "It is Rachel's first!" he proclaimed. "God has opened her womb!"

She was coddled. No longer did my sister go to the fields. Instead, Jacob kept her on a special couch, so she could lounge while Bilhah, Zilpah, and I worked.

In vain, I told him, "Childbearing is natural. A woman doesn't have to be cosseted. She should not lie around for the whole time."

"Rachel is different," he insisted. "We must not take chances."

It was unfair and too much to bear that my sister received such special treatment. The boys were forbidden to play loudly around her and the only thing she was allowed to do was light sewing. When I, too, became pregnant, I raged in silence because no one saw anything wrong with my continued trips to the market and well. I think they barely noticed that my belly was enlarging. As her time drew near, Rachel became increasingly demanding.

"Leah." How I dreaded hearing my name on her lips. Invariably, she wanted something. "My back hurts. Would you rub it?" "Can I have some hummus?" "Could you fluff my pillows?"

It was almost a relief when she began to labor. On and on it dragged. The midwife was concerned. She made Rachel walk around in hopes of speeding-up the process. My sister moaned pathetically and insisted that she couldn't move. The sun set and the moon rose. The sun started his journey again before Rachel's son was born.

"He will be called Joseph," she panted. "I pray the gods add to me more sons."

Jacob knelt at Rachel's side looking from his wife's exhausted face to the little wrinkled face of his newest son. "Rachel, my love, we have a son." Standing with his son in his arms, he proclaimed, "This child is a gift from the God of my Fathers, great and holy is He. He has opened the womb of Rachel just as he did Sarah's and my mother Rebekah's. So, He shows His mighty power. Thus does the One God fulfill his promise to his servants. Joseph, my son, your days will be spent in service to God and He will bring you greatness and honor. Blessed be the God of Abraham and Isaac, the Fear of Jacob who even here, far from my home, has blessed me and opened the womb of my wife to bear me a son!"

I stood in stunned silence. My six sons and the four sons of the servant women were as nothing. Looking at Bilhah and Zilpah, I saw that they had taken an attitude of prayer. Heads lowered and hands crossed on their breast, they listened to Jacob's words. Angry feelings mounted up inside me. Even Reuben, the first-born, had not been greeted with such joy and words of blessing. Unable to bear the sight of the man parading around the room with the baby, I gathered a pile of cloths and slipped from the room.

The midwife followed, eager to share the experience at the next bedside. "It is truly a blessing from the gods that your sister gave birth to such a strong boy after the long labor."

"Yes," my clipped word didn't give much encouragement, but she continued.

"Surely, Jacob has reason for his joy." She peered at me as I handed her the outer garment. "You would think it was his first son," she probed.

Tight lipped, I nodded, holding in my anger with difficulty. I busied myself with folding the blanket I held so that she wouldn't see my real feelings. Her toothless grin made me want to slap her. I knew she understood my silence and that before the day was over all Haran would know that Rachel was again the favored one and Leah was jealous.

Laban entered as the midwife left.

"You have a grandson," I said in response to his questioning look.

"Rachel?" The concern in his voice had me gritting my teeth.

"Is exhausted," I stated, "but joyful that a strong son is born."

Stiffly, I led the way to Rachel's room. Drawing aside the curtain for my father, I saw Jacob again kneeling at Rachel's side as she offered the infant her breast.

Looking up, the woman called, "Father, come and see my son. He will be called Joseph."

"Truly the gods have been gracious." He held the boy in his big hands. "A healthy child has been born to the house of Jacob. The gods will make him great!" Laban handed the whimpering boy back to Rachel, "He wants his mother now."

"Come, my father." Jacob clapped the man on his shoulder. "We will drink health and greatness to my son."

After taking the wineskin to the men, I wandered into the kitchen, cradling my own belly. Jealous anger surged through me for I knew that this child of mine would not be so gladly welcomed.

"Laban and Jacob are celebrating," I told Zilpah. "There will be no need for a meal tonight."

"Truly there is cause to rejoice," she ventured, "your sister is no longer barren, but has born a strong son."

"They are acting as though there has never been another son born. To Joseph belong all the blessings of all the gods." I heard the bitterness in my voice. "None of the others now matter. Even Reuben, Jacob's firstborn, is forgotten." Virulent words poured out until I was sobbing. Then Zilpah took me in her arms. Silently, she rocked me. Jingling bells and boyish shouts told me that the flocks had returned home. In a few minutes I was the mother again, surrounded by the sons of Jacob.

Zilpah smiled. "He won't be able to forget his other children for long," she told me. I had to smile at the boys' clamor and her words. However, in my heart, I knew even then that Joseph had stolen Jacob's heart from his other sons.

My own labor in mid-summer was short and barely noticed by Jacob. The child was a girl. I named her Dinah and reveled in her tiny hands and feet and dimpled mouth. The dark curls that covered her head thrilled me, for I knew she would have lovely hair to match the huge brown eyes that trustingly looked at the world. With a smile for everyone, she was the darling of the household. All her brothers adored her and brought her presents from their wanderings in the fields.

Laban came to the house often. "Let me see my grandsons," he called eagerly. His standard greeting caused a scramble of boyish feet.

Reuben, tall at seven, always led the way and was closely followed by chubby Levi, who, even at five, knew that Grandpa had sweets in his robe. Simeon pushed his way into the circle, his unruly black hair sticking out in all directions. He reminded me of a porcupine, and his personality, too, was prickly. He loved to play tricks on his brothers. Five-year old Dan hurried in dragging Judah on one side and his brother Napthali on the other. Gad, as usual, trailed behind. I admired Dan's care of his brothers. Although he was only a year older, he assumed care of the three half-brothers. The four were seldom apart. Asher and Issachar, my son and Zilpah's, were also usually together. The three-year-olds ran in with their faces covered in something sticky, but with their hands ready for any treat that their grandfather would have. Zebulon squirmed in my arms until I put him down. He rapidly crawled to his grandfather. The ten joined their voices in the clamor around my father.

"Here you are." He crouched to their level and dispensed the sticky sweets.

"Father, you spoil them," I remonstrated with a smile. "Your own children did not get such treats."

"True, but these are my grandsons." Standing back up, he asked, "Where is my newest grandson? Where is Rachel's son?"

I led the way to where Rachel lay like a queen. Even now, months after the birth, she had not resumed the few household tasks that she did.

"Your husband has been richly blessed by this God of his. I, too, have prospered from his care of my flocks," he proclaimed as we walked down the hall. "Eleven healthy sons have been born in this household."

"His time of service for Rachel is complete," I reminded him, ignoring the fact that he didn't mention Dinah at all.

"True." He pursed his lips. "I must speak to him. We will talk later over a skin of wine. I would hate to lose the blessing of his presence and care of my flocks," he confided in a low tone as we entered Rachel's room.

The two men talked late into the night. I caught snippets of the conversation as I took in trays of food and replenished the wine. When Laban finally left, he looked satisfied and I wondered what deal he had talked Jacob into.

"Leah, my wife," my husband called me to his side, "hear what has been decided between your father and myself."

He, too, looked satisfied as he continued. "My time of service for my brides is at an end. Laban has seen how his flocks and herds have prospered under my care. Because of this, we have agreed that from now on, any animal that is not solid in color will be counted as mine. Every solid colored animals will be his. In this way there can be no possibility of cheating."

"Aren't solid colored animals more common?" I asked.

"That is what your father thinks. The God of my Fathers has shown me that this is the way to gain my own herds. Do not be afraid."

"You have a plan," I challenged.

The smile on his face as he leaned back was confirmation; although, all he said was, "Perhaps!"

I wanted to clap my hands, for it seemed that Laban might finally have met his match.

"Tomorrow we will separate the flocks. Laban's solid colored animals will be under my care with his servants. The animals with markings will be under the care of my sons and servants. It is time Simeon and Reuben began to learn to tend the flocks by themselves. We will put my flocks a day and a half on the east of Haran and your father's a day and half journey to the western pastures. Then there can be no claims of trickery."

None of us slept that night. Jacob led the way to Rachel's room where he continued to explain how his herds would grow. "At breeding time, I will put peeled branches in the water troughs when the stronger animals come to drink. The animals will mate at the troughs and their lambs will be multi-colored." Rachel and I stared at the man in amazement. He chuckled, "Your father thinks he has condemned me to having a scant flock of weak animals. The God I serve has promised to give me flocks and herds and wealth along with my sons. When I return to my homeland, all will see that I have been richly blessed. The God of Abraham, Isaac, and my father, Jacob, sent me a dream. All the rams in my dream were spotted and striped. So, has God revealed his promise."

# Chapter 7

The new arrangement worked just as Jacob planned. The lambs born the following spring were indeed strong and healthy. More were mottled than solid colored. Laban was not pleased. I saw him watching my husband many evenings when the animals were driven in to their separate pens.

Time slid by almost unnoticed. The boys grew tall and strong. They were all becoming capable shepherds. Even Zebulon, my youngest son, helped with the sheep. The older boys were in charge of the camels and goats. Only Joseph, toddling about the house followed by Dinah, did not go to the fields. The two handsome children could have been mistaken for twins. They had the same soft brown eyes and wavy brown hair. Their smiles were so much like Jacob's that I sometimes caught my breath when they were laughing together. For Dinah's sake, I was glad that she had inherited the soft curly brown hair of her father and not my straight black hair or even Rachel's glossy auburn waves. Jacob told me that Dinah had my eyes, but I was not sure if I believed him. He took such scant notice of her, I could not believe that he even looked at her eyes.

I learned that sibling rivalry had taken root among the boys. One day I interrupted a wrestling match between Judah and Gad. I scolded my son for taking advantage of his brother's smaller size.

"He's not my real brother," he told me in a whisper.

Appalled, I sat him firmly on the ground. Kneeling to look in his eyes I asked, "Who told you that?"

"Simeon." The dark eyes look at mine innocently.

"We are all one family," I said with a slight shake of his shoulders to emphasize the words.

"Simeon says that we aren't really brothers to Dan and Napthali and Gad and Asher and Joseph," he persisted, trying to convince me.

"You all have the same father," I told him, "and that makes you brothers." I had to force the words out because I, too, wished that Rachel had never offered Bilhah to Jacob and that I had not entered the competition by giving him Zilpah. Looking at my son, I repeated, "You are all brothers. Besides, you should always treat the younger and weaker with kindness."

The boy studied my face with serious intent. At last, he threw his arms around my neck. "I'm sorry, Mother. I'll tell Simeon that he was wrong. I'll be nice to them all."

Returning his hug, I said, "I'll talk to Simeon. Go on and play."

Simeon, my fierce son, was always on the watch for anyone who would steal his rights. I loved him, even though I feared his temper. Like mine, his temper blazed hot at injustice; but, unlike me, he was not afraid to confront the transgressor and demand his rights. I drew him aside later in the evening.

"My son." I paused, unable to find the words that had seemed so clear in the afternoon.

"Yes, my mother?" he replied, leaning against the wall in his six year-old imitation of a man.

"Simeon, why did you tell Judah that Dan and Gad, Napthali, Asher, and Joseph are not his brothers?" I decided the direct approach was best.

He tilted his chin and I saw his fists clench in the dimming light. "They aren't." His young voice held conviction.

"Your father is their father. That makes you all brothers," I pointed out putting my hand over his fist.

"You aren't their mother. They are not my brothers." The repeated words sprang from his desire to protect me. "You have to take care of them and never get to have fun or play with the sheep."

"Simeon," I gathered the stiffly outraged boy into my arms, "I love to care for you boys much more than I could ever care for sheep and goats."

"Really?" The surprise took his mind off the subject, but only for a second.

"I don't think you should have to take care of them. They are not my real brothers."

"My son," I held his face between my hands, "they are indeed your brothers. For better or worse, you must live with them as brothers."

His pout and defiant eyes told me that he still did not believe me. "For you, I will count them as brothers." His words sounded old for his age as he stubbornly continued, "But, I will not think of them as brothers."

I heard in his words the echo of Sarah, wife of Abraham the Wanderer, 'The son of the slave girl shall not inherit with my son'. From girlhood I had heard how Abraham was forced to send his first-born son away after Isaac was born because of Sarah's jealousy.

Unable to think of a response, I watched the small boy march proudly into the house. I sat staring at the rising moon for a long time, knowing in my heart that I wanted to say the same thing about the sons of the maids and even about Rachel's son.

One afternoon I sat carding wool in the courtyard. Joseph and Dinah, still inseparable at nearly four, had found a nest. Built on a low branch of the shade tree in the courtyard, they could sit on the wall and see into it. Silently, they sat staring in awe, lost in the world of the tiny chirping inhabitants of the nest.

Laban's voice was heard asking for me. One of the new slave girls answered softly. I marveled briefly about the wealth that Jacob was accumulating. Not only were his flocks growing with the multi-colored lambs as designated, but also he was able to sell the animals at great profit for they were so healthy. We had camels and goats and sheep. Every year he obtained more servants and slaves. In just the last two years, new pens had to be constructed, as well as an addition to the house for the new household and field attendants.

I rose to greet my father, wondering why he would be coming to see me in the middle of the day. "Where is Jacob?" he demanded gruffly.

"In the fields with his sons and Rachel." The answer didn't please the man.

"I have to talk to him." He began to pace. I saw the children frown slightly as his steps took him toward the tree. The mother bird fluttered anxiously up from the nest.

"Come inside," I urged. "When the sun goes down, Jacob will return."

"He should be here now! I sent for him to come." The tone made me concerned.

"Is something wrong?" I asked. "My brothers?"

"Your brothers are being cheated," he stated, "that is what is wrong."

Surprised, I started to speak, but Jacob's arrival made me shut my mouth.

Circling his son-in-law, Laban angrily accused him of stealing. "You were to keep only those animals that showed white markings in the dark fur," he shouted.

Standing face to face, the two men resembled tomcats circling for an advantage. Trying to remain calm, Jacob replied, "Father of my wives, again you change my wage. We agreed not even a year ago that all the animals with any striping would belong in my herd. Before that you swore that the mottled animals were to be mine."

Laban puffed his chest and cheeks in rage. Then he huffed, "You have tricked me. Your herds increase and mine decrease. Your animals are strong and mine are weak."

"Father Laban," Jacob offered a conciliatory hand on the shoulder. "I cannot but repeat what you yourself have said."

The man shrugged off the hand, interrupting, "Yes, yes, 'the One God blesses all you do', so you say. I think there is more." His eyes narrowed as he looked at his nephew. Then my father turned to me.

"Leah, daughter, what magic does this man use to force the sheep and goats to bear whatever color I set as his wage?"

"I am not a shepherd," I responded, "only a humble woman. Perhaps the God of my husband is indeed blessing Jacob with flocks. He has also blessed my husband with many children." I glanced toward where the two youngest were again quietly absorbed in the bird family.

Laban followed my gaze and he nodded grudgingly. Turning to my husband, he said, "It is true that your god has given you sons and even opened the womb of my daughter Rachel to bear you a fine son."

The discussion resumed more amicably as Jacob replied, "Father Laban, I will honor your request. My herds will only be increased by any animal with a white spot or stripe in their coat. Solid animals will remain yours."

"Also, those with dark spots and stripes," Laban added, holding out his hand.

Jacob took the offered hand and nodded, "Agreed, let us seal the new deal and ask the blessing of God over both our herds."

I hurried to bring a skin of wine, knowing that the men would now talk and boast long into the night. Later, after all the boys were safely tucked into their beds and Dinah slept contentedly on the mat in my room, I pondered my words. "God has indeed blessed my husband," I whispered. "The One God has even blessed me on Jacob's behalf. Though I do not have my husband's love, I have the love of his sons and Dinah." Overwhelmed by the realization of such bounty from a god, I knelt and wept softly. Briefly, I caught a glimpse of the love that surrounded me. In the months that followed, I often wished for the serenity of that moment.

Again and again, Laban changed Jacob's share of the flock. Again and again, the One God blessed and multiplied my husband's herds. My brothers and my father grew angrier and angrier. The tension was unbearable when the men met on the roads of Haran. I was afraid that more than angry words would result from each encounter.

# Chapter 8

"Come with me to the fields." Jacob's words came as a surprise one spring morning.

Rachel and I looked at each other and shrugged. Calling to Dinah and Joseph, we followed Jacob. The older boys had already driven the animals to the fields where the first grasses were starting to edge up through the cool ground. After a long tramp, Jacob stopped. He leaned against a tall rock. Rachel and I found a convenient boulder to use as a seat. The children scampered off to explore a likely looking pile of stones.

"My wives," Jacob began. He looked toward the eastern mountains and then back at us. "The God of my fathers has come to me. It is time to return to my homeland." Rachel and I looked at each other, wondering what he meant. "You know how your father has tried to trick me," he continued, still with the faraway look in his eyes. "Laban has changed my wages ten times in the past six years. The God of my fathers has been with me to protect and bless me." A small smile formed as he remembered Laban's frustration. "If the wages were to be spotted animals, that is what the herds bore. When he changed to striped, then all the lambs were striped." The man looked at us. "Rachel, my love, and Leah, my wife, it is time for me to return to the land of Canaan. I want to see my father and make peace with my brother." He held out his hands almost in supplication.

Rachel took one hand. She kissed the palm and then held it to her cheek.

My response was more practical. "If your God has told you to return to Canaan, your home, then we must go."

"You would leave your father and Haran, all you know, to come with me?" Jacob's reply was edged with surprise and the smile he gave me was pleased.

Not to be outdone, Rachel took hold of his hands, "My husband, my love, what has my father to do with me now? All that he kept from my dowry has been spent. The profit he obtained from your work is used up."

Ignoring Rachel's exclusion of me, I mentioned, "Tomorrow, Laban and my brothers will be going to the far pasture for the shearing."

Jacob laughed, "What a schemer you are, Leah, my wife! That is the perfect excuse for us to leave also. Who would question that I would take my sons and wives with me to shear my own flocks? We will leave with the sunrise day after tomorrow."

"There is much to be done." Ever practical, I didn't allow myself to revel in my husband's approving smile for long.

"Yes." His thoughts turned to the animals. "I must gather the flocks and herds together on the far side of Haran. The camels will be used by the women and youngest children."

My mind was already busy arranging what would be packed and what would be left behind. "Come Rachel," I said as I tugged her arm brusquely, "there is much to do."

Sighing irritably, she called to Joseph. He came, followed by Dinah. They were both dusty and hungry from the morning outing. The house became a whirlwind of activity throughout the evening and next day. All the servants were set to baking and packing. From the door, I waved to my father as he set out toward the west to shear his flocks. A twinge of guilt was quickly suppressed by reminding myself of the many times he had tried to cheat Jacob. My loyalty and love rest with the father of my children.

Late in the afternoon, I saw Rachel hurrying back from Laban's house. She carried a bundle wrapped in a veil that I recognized.

"What have you done?" I confronted my sister in her room.

Defiantly, she stood between the roll lying on her blankets and me.

"Do you plan to bring danger and death to us all?" I whispered.

"Not danger, but protection," she replied. Her strength surprised me as she held me off when I tried to reach around her.

"Are not Jacob and his God protection enough for you?"

Rachel ignored my challenge. She turned and unwrapped first one, then a second and a third of Laban's household gods. For as long as I could remember, these little stone figures had resided in the alcove in my father's house. The curtain they now lay on had covered the opening, except when he made offerings. Like all in Haran, Laban believed that the household gods protected the house and all in it. Each family had their own favorite gods and inheritance was proven by possession of the gods. Jacob had never allowed any of the figures in our home. The man explained that the One God is everywhere and cannot be represented by a statue or contained in an alcove.

"Jacob will be furious!" I turned again to Rachel. "You know he doesn't believe in the gods of Haran."

She pouted, "He won't know if you don't tell him. Besides," tears started to brim, "I want a piece of Haran to take with me. Won't you miss all that we've ever known?"

I paused before answering, pondering her words. In all honesty I was excited about leaving. In Haran I was pitied.

Perhaps somewhere new I would find respect, if not love, from my husband. "I don't know. I have never been away from Haran. My trust is in my husband and his God. The God that blessed Jacob with sons and flocks will not abandon him now. There is no need for our father's gods."

Stubbornly, she lifted her chin, "Jacob need not know," she repeated. "What harm can they do?"

I opened my mouth to explain. A crash followed by the crying of a child sent us both running from the room. The young son of one of the new servant girls had toppled a pile of pottery. He was crying more from fear than injury.

"He did not mean to do it. There is no harm done. Go on with your work," I told the girl as she rushed in to snatch her son.

Distracted by the crisis, I forgot my sister's theft. I didn't see the incriminating bundle when the camels were loaded in the dim morning light and decided she had returned the idols. With the sound of camel complaints and the jangling of harnesses, we set out. Jacob tossed random greetings to curious faces in doorways. He left the impression that, like Laban, he had decided to make the sheep shearing a family event. We reached the flocks by midmorning. Reuben, Simeon, and Levi were proud of their new responsibility. Each was in charge of a third of the animals. With their brothers, they already had the animals grazing steadily eastward and south along the valley toward the river crossing. Even Zebulon at eight was happily assisting with the herding. Proudly, I looked at my sturdy and handsome sons.

"They grow up so quickly," I mused to Zilpah that evening. Watching Jacob and his sons erect a tent made me realize that Reuben would soon be a man. Already his chest was broadening and his voice sometimes took on a deeper tone. Could it have been thirteen years earlier when I bore

Jacob's first son? I ached when I saw the attention lavished on Joseph that my sons never received from their father.

"They are all your sons, equally important. Joseph is no more special than Reuben or Judah or any of your children." In vain, I argued again and again in the five years since Joseph was born. Seeing Jacob working side by side with his sons, I hoped he would see their value too.

A week slid by on the steady rocking of the camels. Rapidly, we traveled South and West each day. During the day, the animals were kept moving with barely a pause for water. Each night, we made camp on a high point and the flocks grazed below and around the camp. The scenery changed after we crossed the Euphrates.

I told stories of Abraham the Wanderer to Joseph and Dinah. "Like Abraham, we are traveling at the command of the One God," I told them. "He came from far away to the south of Haran and then traveled even further away, even as far as Egypt, before settling in Canaan. That is where we are going. Canaan, where your father was born."

Travel slowed as we passed the city of Damascus and reached the first hills of Canaan. I noticed that Jacob kept looking back from the higher ridges. We reached the hills of Gilead in only ten days and he announced, "We will camp here for a day. The animals need rest. There is rich pasture here in the shelter of these hills."

Several tents were erected instead of the single one we had been using for the past week. I was not surprised when he insisted that all the boys remain in camp or that the animals were pastured on the far side of the camp.

"You expect Laban to follow?" I confronted my husband as he stood alone looking to the north.

"Perhaps." He barely glanced at me. His eyes were intent on the puff of smoke on the horizon. It grew into a cloud of dust and men as it approached. "Go to your tent and take your sons," he demanded.

Reuben and Simeon insisted that they were old enough to stand with their father until he turned and commanded, "Go and protect the women!"

Proudly, they strutted to my tent. I wanted to hug and scold them. Staunchly, they took their stand in front of the tent. Rachel took Joseph into her tent. Bilhah and Zilpah also went to their tents with their sons. The other women and children crowded into the remaining shelter. I felt the tension in the camp as the men took their stand behind Jacob. Watching, I understood that Jacob had planned this location well.

Laban was on the lower ground and at a disadvantage. He stopped to challenge his son-in-law. "Why did you run away?" The angry voice carried across the distance between the two men. "You did not let me say goodbye to my daughters and grandsons."

Jacob leaned on his staff. He appeared unconcerned by the armed mass of men facing him. Behind my father and brothers were all Laban's servants as well as many of the men of Haran. "I feared you would not let your daughters go with me. My God has commanded me to return to my homeland. The One God has called me to make peace with my father and my twin."

My brothers made sounds of derision and a murmur arose from their followers. Each man shifted his weapon so that the sun glinted on the metal points. I held my breath. A word from my father and combat would be joined.

"Your God." For once Laban did not sneer at the words. He started to speak, stopped, and then continued. "Your God came to me in the night and warned me not to curse you or to harm you."

Silence greeted his statement. Jacob stared steadily at the man who was his relation by blood and marriage. Laban looked away first. I saw Jacob sigh in relief, but my father was not through. "If you have the protection of your God, why did you steal my household gods?"

The look of shock and astonishment on Jacob's face should have been proof of his innocence even before he waved his arm to the camp. "I took nothing of yours except what was mine by labor. I brought your daughters, my wives, and the flocks I have earned despite changes in my wages. Search this camp! Show me what I took of yours! Place it here before your men and my people! Let them judge between us!" The man was raging at the end of the speech. With a wave of his staff, Jacob indicated the camp was open to Laban's inspection.

Signaling his men to wait, Laban dismounted and stamped forward. The baggage of the men was easily searched, lying open beside the fire. Then he turned to the tents. Without a word or nod, my father searched through my bags and then in Bilhah's and Zilpah's belongings. The children stood silent before his frown. None clamored for sweetmeats. They all felt the tension and anger in the camp. Dinah whimpered in fright by my side.

Laban threw back the flap on Rachel's tent. She sat calmly on her camel's saddle. "My lord father." She greeted him with a smile that he did not return. Feverishly now, he searched her bundles but found no gods. My heart was in my throat when he turned to his daughter. With a winsome smile, she said, "Do not be angry that I don't get up. You see it is my woman's time."

Laban's face showed his frustration and embarrassment. Empty handed he emerged from Rachel's tent.

Jacob shouted his challenge from the hill he still stood on. "Show me what you found! Which of your household goods have you found in my camp? Place the stolen items here!" He pointed to the ground between his servants and the men of Haran.

"I found nothing." The reply came grudgingly as my father held up empty hands.

"Then you admit that you have wronged me again?" My husband's voice rang out. " I worked fourteen years to wed your two daughters. Then, I tended your flocks and herds another six years for my own animals. Yet, your animals have not miscarried. The loss of either flock I bore whether from wild animals or weakness. In that time, you changed my wages ten times. If it were not for the protection of the One God, the God of Abraham and the Fear of my father Isaac, I should have left your household with less than I arrived with. Yet, the God of my fathers has rebuked you."

He paused to take a breath and Laban raised his hand. It was a motion of surrender. "Enough, I did not find my gods in your baggage. My daughters and their children are still my concern. You should not take them into danger. Who knows how your brother will welcome you? It may well be he will kill you and my children will be left bereft and alone in a foreign land."

Jacob tossed his head in haughty anger. I saw his servants lay hands on their weapons and held my breath. By custom, he would be within his rights to strike down Laban for his false accusations. Instead, he offered peace. "Laban, your allegations are false." The words hung between my father and my husband. "You have continually cheated me of my rightful wages. Now you seek to remove my wives and children from me." He spoke slowly and clearly. After a moment of silence, Jacob added, "Your daughters are my wives, my sons are your grandsons." He ignored the restless murmurs and movement in the ranks of men behind and facing him. I was proud of my husband's next suggestion.

"Let us set up a pillar before God and these witnesses that there may be peace between us."

Silently, nephew and uncle stared at each other. Time seemed suspended. Not even a child's giggle or cry broke the quiet. The rustle of some man's restless feet echoed loudly and the clink of metal against metal sounded a discord.

Finally, Laban spoke. "Jacob, son of Isaac of Canaan, you are wise beyond your years. Let it be as you say. We will set up a pillar as witness between you and me."

Each man turned and gave an order for stones to be set up as a pillar to mark the boundary treaty between Jacob and Laban. Weapons sheathed but at their sides, the men brought rocks to the hill where my husband made his stand.

"We must prepare food," I said. "Reuben, go to the flock and fetch two lambs for sacrifice and two kids for roasting."

Bilhah and Zilpah set to work with the other women making the flat bread and preparing the humus and bean curd. I sent the other children to gather fresh herbs from the hills. To protect her lie, Rachel had to stay in her tent, but I put her to work polishing the platters with sand and arranging the dried fruits we had. She pouted but did not argue. I saw that she was as relieved as I that there had not been a fight.

By the time the men gathered at the completed monument, the covenant meal was completed. Jacob and Laban stood on opposite sides of the mound of stones. Their servants and kinsmen gathered at their backs. We women and children stood at the edge of the camp to watch.

Laban spoke first. "Let this pillar and these stones be called Garsahadutha as a witness between Jacob, son of Isaac of Canaan and Laban, son of Nahor the Aramean of Haran. May the gods watch between us."

Jacob replied, "These stones raised as a boundary marker will be known as Galeed and this pillar of treaty called Mizpah, for it will be a watch post between Laban the

Aramean of Haran and Jacob of Canaan, son of Isaac. The God of Abraham and Isaac will be the security."

I heard my father warn, "This pillar is indeed a watch post. Know that indeed your God and my gods are witness between you and me. Remember this," he said as a threat, "if you desire other wives or mistreat my daughters the gods will judge you. They can see where man cannot."

"So be it," Jacob responded with a salaam to his father-in-law. The sun was starting its descent when Jacob turned and took the lamb for the sacrifice. My brother Cabel held the other lamb. Joshih stood beside Laban with the fire ready to kindle the offering. "May the God of Abraham the Wanderer, the God and Fear of Isaac my father be judge and witness between us."

Everyone fell prostrate as the blood of the sacrifice was sprinkled on the pillar and stones sealing the agreement. I saw the final blazing light of the sun strike the pillar when Jacob laid the lamb on the stones and bowed to the ground. The other lamb was also killed, and Laban lit the wood. The sacrificial fire merged with the sun's fading light. Fire consumed the offering and the covenant was made to keep peace between my father and my husband. It seemed a fitting end to the day.

The men rose when the sun disappeared. Jacob signaled that it was time for the feast to seal the treaty. The men all sat down around the monument. The women brought bread, meat, and vegetables for the meal. I carried a skin of wine to Jacob. He poured a cup and handed it to Laban. Laban poured a cup and handed it to his son-in-law. They drank to the cheers of the assembled men. Then all hands reached for the food. Bilhah and Zilpah filled the men's cups with wine and then we all left the men to their celebration.

Morning came too soon. Laban waited for me to bring his grandchildren. With tears, he hugged and blessed each boy. A final sweetmeat and kiss was given. Five year old Joseph stared at his grandfather with wide eyes. Laban took him by the shoulders when Rachel led him to her father.

"Joseph, the God of your father has destined you for greatness. Those who are born to the barren are doubly blessed. Learn well your lessons. Perhaps you will return to Haran as a great man someday." I had to grit my teeth against angry words. My father had not suggested that any of the other boys would return to Haran. Laban kissed both Rachel and me before turning to Jacob with a warning and reminder.

"These rocks are a witness that no one of mine will pass to the south nor will you or yours travel to the north of it. May your God prosper your journey. The gods will watch between us."

Then my father turned and headed back to Haran leading my brothers and his men. I watched with sorrow, knowing I would never see my family again.

# Chapter 9

We traveled south. No longer was Jacob pushing the men and flocks to great distances each day. Every day brought new sights. Some wonderful rock or a small animal or insect that was skillfully captured was shared with me by my sons. Even Dinah roamed happily with her brothers watching her. She braided flower chains for me and for her aunt and even for Zilpah and Bilhah. Rachel insisted that Joseph stay close to the camel caravan where we women rode serenely, high above the dust raised by the flocks.

"He will be perfectly safe with his brothers," I urged nearly every morning. His longing look when his half brothers headed off to the flocks and fields almost broke my heart. Sometimes Dinah relented and stayed with him but she preferred to explore with her brothers.

Rachel looked fearfully around at the strange and unfamiliar hills. She shook her head. "They might forget him and he could get lost or hurt."

"Dinah has come to no harm," I reminded my sister.

Stubbornly, she shook her head. She looked at her only son. He sat by the fire sadly nibbling a piece of bread while Zebulon and Issachar talked about an interesting outcropping they planned to explore.

"I do not dare risk the precious gift from the gods. He must be kept separate and safe from danger."

"You may well lose him by holding him too tightly." My warning was ignored.

"Mother, even Reuben and Simeon have permission to leave the flocks and go." The boy stood before his mother pointing to his older brothers.

Still Rachel shook her head. "No." Her voice was surprisingly firm.

"Even Dinah is going." The boy darted a glance toward the group forming near the fire. "She's just a girl and younger than me." His voice took on a pleading singsong tone.

"Joseph!" His mother's voice was sharp. "You will obey me! I do not want to hear what the others are doing. You are special," she softened the words with a smile and held out her hand. "Stay with me and I will tell you a story."

Tearfully, Joseph appealed to his father. "Can't I go with my brothers?"

Jacob paused in his walk through the camp. "My son," he tousled the boy's curly brown hair. I hoped he was going to agree. Rachel sprang up with a cry.

"No!" She caught Jacob's arm and looked up into his eyes. "Let not my husband be angry with the lad's impertinence. He is too young to go so far."

Shaking my head at her obstinate refusal, I walked away toward the ten boys. I knew that Jacob would give in to his beloved Rachel. I felt sorry for the child.

"Is Joseph coming?" Levi called impatiently. My sons were ready to set out. Gad and Judah held Dinah's hand. She danced with excitement.

I shook my head, "I don't think so." A quick glance at my husband caught him shaking his head at Joseph. His hand caressed Rachel's cheek. I watched Joseph, hoping he would have the courage to disobey. Instead, he ran into the tent. His mother hurried after him.

"Go on and explore. Bring me news of all that you find." Forcing a cheerful note into my voice I sent the children off.

Watching them troop from the camp, I wished I could be one of the group. Distantly, I heard Joseph's sobs and Rachel cajoling him. I saw Jacob stride out to the flocks.

It was late in the afternoon when, dusty and tired, the group returned to camp. Simeon carried Dinah on his shoulders. Triumphant she held a bunch of wilted wildflowers for me. Her brothers all tried to talk at once. I caught only bits of the conversation.

"Piles of rocks ..."

"It was really high."

"... animal tracks."

Joseph stood sadly in the tent opening. I held out my hand in invitation but he shook his head and ducked back inside. They repeated the day's adventures for their father during dinner. Joseph sat quiet but his eyes held a longing to be like his brothers. I resolved to talk to his father, but the opportunity was lost. After the children stumbled off to bed, Jacob spoke.

"I have had word that my brother Esau is coming this way. He has four hundred armed men with him."

Rachel gasped and grabbed his arm.

With a self-deprecating smile, he continued, "I guess he is still angry about the stolen blessing."

"You must send him an offering, a gift," I suggested.

"That is my plan. We will leave here in the morning. I will send ahead of us a series of gifts as to a king."

Rachel clung to his arm. "What if he is not appeased?"

"The God of Abraham and Isaac told me to return home. He will not desert me now," the man replied with assurance.

"What are you sending?" I asked more to divert my sister's fear than from curiosity.

He started to detail the animals. "First, I will send two hundred female goats and twenty males. Then ..."

Rachel interrupted, "Why so many?"

"Lovely Rachel, I shall not leave us destitute. However, I will lavish my brother with gifts." Then he added, "Each man is instructed to tell Esau, 'This is a gift from my lord Jacob. He is behind me.' "

I couldn't help but smile. "He cannot but wonder at your generosity. I'm sure you have given thought to the fact that the multitude of animals may be some hindrance to his march."

Jacob grinned boyishly. "Sly Leah, I had not thought of that." Then he added seriously, "I do owe my brother an apology. Even all my flocks and herds will never fully repay him for our father's blessing which I stole." He stood up to pace. I could tell that he was troubled.

"May your God grant you reconciliation," I whispered the prayer.

I slept little, my mind turning over and over between prayer and worry about the coming meeting. The herd of goats left when the sun was barely a hint on the horizon. Two hundred ewes and twenty rams departed as the boys rose and ate their morning bread. Jacob oversaw the striking of camp as the flock of camels moved south. Our riding camels were ready when forty cows and ten bulls set out. Then, the final group of twenty female and ten male donkeys left the camp to meet Esau. At last, the main herd started. Rachel and I were cozily settled on our camels. Jacob and his sons walked with the herds. Joseph rode with his mother. Dinah, still tired from her adventure the day before, was happy to doze in my arms.

I heard Rachel tell her son again, "See how important you are. No walking in the dust for the favorite son of Jacob bar Isaac. You will never need to walk in the dust or work with your hands. Your father's God has destined you for greatness."

Angrily, I ground my teeth and urged my camel past Rachel's so I didn't have to listen to her filling the boy's head with nonsense. "All of Jacob's sons are great," I told myself. "He knew that before my sister had her son. It is not fair that they should be second best now." Again, I resolved to speak to Jacob.

The late afternoon sun was in our eyes as we descended to the little trickle of water called Jabok. After living near the birthplace of the Euphrates all my life, the rivers of Canaan seemed mere brooks. The Euphrates tumbled out of the mountains already a strong current. I had heard stories about how it grew and grew as it flowed south, becoming a mighty waterway for boats and watering the whole of Sumeria. These streams barely watered the land on each side.

Jacob paced restlessly along the bank, looking to the south where there was richer grazing and higher ground. "You will all cross tonight," he announced when he finally joined us. "The grass is better on the other side." His order sent the servants to herding the animals across the stream. "I will stay on this side and pray tonight."

"Can't we stay too?" Reuben and Simon looked hopefully at their father.

"No, my sons." His smile was weary. "I seek God's direction this night—alone. You will be needed with the women and flocks. They are in your charge."

Proudly, my sons straightened their backs. I wondered if they heard the unspoken command to defend us if he should not return.

"You can depend on us Father," Simeon stated and Reuben nodded. Jacob placed a hand on each boy's shoulder. They were of a height with one another and able to look their father in the eye.

"I know that. You are good shepherds, good sons."

Proud of their father's approbation, the boys ran to join the servants and finish the crossing.

Jacob turned to Rachel and Joseph. He drew them together into his embrace. "Rachel, my love, and Joseph, beloved son," he kissed each face, "cross the Jabok and make camp. I will come in the morning."

Then one at a time he kissed each of his sons. He gave every boy a special task in the camp. For a minute, I thought he would not kiss me. He stood watching Rachel and Joseph cross the brook. Bilhah and Zilpah followed with the other seven boys. Dinah was holding tight to Levi's hand and laughing at something that he said. Still I stood beside my camel. With resignation I took up the lead rope to follow my sister and my sons.

"Leah." My name on his lips stopped me. I felt his hands on my shoulders as he turned me to face him. "Leah, I am seeking God tonight. I want His assurance before I enter Canaan. If I do not survive the meeting," he paused to take a deep breath, "you, my faithful wife, will bring my family to Isaac."

There were many things I wanted to say. I wanted to tell him of my love and beg him not to risk meeting the One God. The words refused to be spoken. Looking into his eyes I knew that my husband, Jacob son of Isaac and grandson of Abraham the Wanderer, was set on demanding answers from his God. Instead of words, I lifted his hand to press a kiss onto the palm.

"Leah, do not be afraid," he told me with a kiss on the forehead and a half smile.

"I'm not." I shook my head. "Your God has not brought you here to strike you down. May the God of Abraham and Isaac bless you and give you your desire. I pray you will find the answers you seek."

"Leah.." He started to say something, so I paused at the water's edge to look back. He was standing very alone, staring at me. When he didn't speak, I raised one hand and turned to cross the brook.

Camp was well on the way to being set-up when I reached it. Rachel hurried to meet me.

"What did Jacob tell you?" I heard a touch of jealousy in her voice.

"He is demanding answers from his God tonight," I replied, looking over my shoulder. In the last light of the setting sun we could see the man moving toward the rocky outcropping and starting to climb. "He will join us in the morning," I added. "Now we must feed the children and servants."

I slipped out of my tent after everyone was sleeping. The air was still. Not even a night creature stirred. In the silence of the sleeping camp, I tiptoed to the water's edge to keep vigil. I could see nothing on the other side of the river. No moon rose to give light to the pitch-black night. The stars seemed cold and far away. I felt my husband's loneliness as he awaited his God. My heart breathed a prayer. "God of Jacob, my husband seeks you this night. Be merciful and gracious to him. You have blessed him with wealth and sons. Please favor him with your assurance now."

All through the night I crouched beside the Jabok. Eventually, the first rays of the morning sun were streaking the hills. I strained my eyes to see across the brook. There was no movement. Fear clutched my throat but still I waited. When the rising sun lit up the camp and resting herds, I saw a figure limping toward the water. The sun in my eyes prevented me from seeing his face, but I knew the man. "Jacob." I breathed the name even as I rushed to greet him. My husband was the same, but he was different, too. He was limping and seemed unconcerned that he trailed his robe behind him. The tunic he wore was dusty. As we drew closer together, I saw that his hair and beard were full of dirt and twigs. It was his eyes that caught my attention. A strange light burned in them. The man stopped when I reached him. Tentatively, I reached up to take a twig from his beard.

He caught my hand tightly in both his. "I have spent the night with God." The awe in his voice kept me quiet for a minute.

"What is God like?" I asked when he didn't continue.

"I wrestled with God." Jacob turned to look back across the Jabok. "God has blessed me." He took a deep breath and looked toward the camp. He seemed hesitant to return to the normal life of shepherd and father. "Leah, God has given me a new name. Just as he renamed Abram to become Abraham." He reclaimed my hands and spoke with such amazement and joy that I felt tears pricking my eyes.

I stared at this man who caused such mixed emotions in my heart. Without a doubt, the hand of God was on him. "Tell me," I urged. Belief in his God was the one common ground with my husband that Rachel did not have. She still did not believe that one god was better than any other.

Sitting on a rock, he drew me down beside him. "I was alone in the darkness. Not even a moon lightened the night." He looked inward at the night just past.

"I know." At his curious look I felt my face redden. "I watched and prayed for you here last night."

A gentle kiss on my forehead signaled his appreciation and approval. The love in that kiss flowed through my body and nestled inside me.

"For a long time I prayed for some sign from God. 'Where are you God?' I shouted to the silence. There seemed to be no answer, just the bleakness of the night. Then, suddenly there was a man standing in front of me." My husband shook his head at the memory. "He asked what I wanted. 'I seek

God', was my answer. He promised to bring me safely home again. I cannot go back to Haran and I dare not go forward because my brother will kill me."

I made a slight sound. Jacob smiled at me and then continued. "'God is with you,' the strange man said. That's when I became angry and stood up." Jacob stopped in the narrative to shake his head at his stupidity. "We stood face to face in the darkness. I couldn't see his face but I knew he was there. 'I want assurance from God himself,' I shouted at the stranger. Then I grabbed this man by the shoulders to thrust him out of my camp. I was sure God would not visit me while this impertinent fellow bothered me. Easily he threw me to the ground. I refused to be defeated and pulled him down with me. We struggled together for hours." Jacob paused to wipe sweat from his brow. Reliving the night was making my heart pound too. "It wasn't until he sprained my hip," with reverence my husband touched his hip at the memory, "that I realized that I was not wrestling with a man or an angel, but with God himself. Still, I refused to let go. 'Bless me,' I begged." I couldn't help the gasp at my husband's impertinence. "It was then that God told me, 'You will no longer be Jacob, the one who supplants. Your name will be Israel, for you have striven with God and with man and prevailed.' When I asked him for his name, he refused to give me an answer, but laid his hands on me in blessing. Then he was gone. I was alone. The sun was starting to come up."

Silent and in awe, I stared at my husband. With his arm around me, we gazed across the brook to the holy place where man and God strove together.

"And Esau?" I ventured, at last returning to the practicalities of the present.

"I will make peace with my brother. Come we must dedicate this crossing. It shall be called Peni-el, for a mere man has seen the face of God. Limping rapidly, Jacob hurried to awaken the camp. The ceremony took half the morning. The sun stood high in the sky when the camels were loaded.

"This is how we will meet Esau," Jacob instructed with his family gathered around. "Zilpah, you will go first with Gad and Asher. Bilhah will follow on the second camel. Dan and Napthali will go with her. Leah, you will be next. Reuben and Simeon with their brothers Levi and Judah will ride donkeys behind you. Issachar and Zebulon will lead the camel and Dinah will ride with you. Finally, Rachel with Joseph will come on the last camel."

Even my amazement at his new status and the shared memories of the night past didn't stop my quick words. "You seek to save Rachel and Joseph even if Esau slaughters all your other sons."

"Leah!" Rachel turned shocked eyes on me. "How can you say such a thing!" She began to sob fearfully.

"That will not happen," Jacob assured her with a kiss, although I saw the passing look of guilt on his face. "I seek peace. That is why I sent the gifts to my brother."

"See!" Rachel nodded triumphantly, no longer crying. "I knew my husband had a good reason."

"I will go ahead of you all," Jacob continued. "I will hold out my hands empty of any weapon to show I come in peace. If necessary, I will grovel to my brother."

# Chapter 10

Jacob dressed in his grandest robes and had us all do the same.

"Giving Esau honor as a potentate may assuage some anger," Jacob said with a wink as he boosted Rachel onto her camel saddle. "Don't be afraid my love."

When he was satisfied with our presentation, my husband set out walking ahead of Zilpah's camel. Her sons led the beast. Bilhah and I followed with my oldest sons trotting beside on their donkeys while Zebulon and Issachar proudly led the camel. Rachel trailed behind us holding Joseph tightly in her arms while a servant led the animal. Behind us, the herds spread out under the control of Jacob's servants to graze slowly as we moved along the road.

We topped a hill and saw Esau's men milling around in the valley. I noted with a slight smile that Jacob's presents were indeed a nuisance. They were distracting the fighting men and I could hear curses on the slight breeze as the warriors tried to form up behind Esau.

Then my eyes turned to the two men drawing closer to one another. "Pray to God he accepts peace," I breathed, clutching Dinah close to my heart. Issachar looked up.

"Mother, will not the God of my father protect him?"

"Yes, he will," I reassured the boy and myself.

Jacob limped toward his brother, stopping every few steps to bow low to the ground in homage, as one would honor the *LuGal* in the capital. Lined up on the hilltop, we could see and hear the meeting only a few yards away. I held my breath when the men came face to face. Esau with his four hundred men faced Jacob who stood alone, save for his family on the hilltop. The remaining men and all the flocks owned by my husband were ordered to stay out of sight. Then Esau held out his hand and raised his brother from the ground to draw him into an embrace. They wept together and I felt tears running down my cheeks too.

"What is this?" Esau's gesture encompassed us.

"The family God has given me much." Jacob's pride was clear in his voice.

With a wave of his hand he signaled us to come forward. First, Zilpah with Gad and Asher were introduced. "My brother, these are my sons Gad and Asher born to Zilpah maidservant to my wife Leah." Patting each boy on the back he told him, "This is your Uncle Esau." Zilpah bowed to the ground and her sons followed her lead.

Before Esau could respond, Bilhah dismounted to bow before the men. Dan and Napthali knelt beside her. "These are my sons by Bilhah, my beloved Rachel's maid. Here is Dan and Napthali."

I felt strangely embarrassed bowing to Jacob's brother. My sons dismounted to follow my lead. "My wife, Leah, and her sons," Jacob's wave of a hand indicated the six boys. One by one they came forward. "Meet your uncle," he ordered as he introduced them. "Reuben is my firstborn, and Simeon is the next born and quite a joker." Jacob smiled at his son. "Levi and Judah were born next." I saw Esau looking from my sons to the maids' sons and assessing their ages. Jacob continued the introductions. "Here are Issachar and Zebulon. They are nearly my youngest sons."

Already he was moving toward Rachel's camel, ignoring Dinah, who was holding my hand. Overwhelmed, Esau stared at his many nephews. My husband lifted my sister from her camel. Hand in hand the couple walked to Esau. Joseph held tight to his mother's hand. "My brother, here is my beloved wife, Rachel, and my youngest son, Joseph. As with our birth and like our father, the One God opened Rachel's womb to bear Joseph." My husband placed a proud hand on the five year-old boy's shoulder. "The hand of God is on this son for great things."

The old hurt rose from my heart to clutch my throat. How dare he set the youngest above his first-born? I saw Reuben's eyebrows draw together. He looked at Simeon whose glare mirrored the hurt and anger at Jacob's thoughtless words.

"God has been gracious to you, my brother," Esau proclaimed, impressed by the multitude of sons and wives he had met. "What do you mean by sending all these animals ahead to me. Surely you need them yourself."

"No, my brother, the God of our father has blessed me. I have flocks and herds enough. Accept the meager gift from my hand as the duty due from a younger son to his elder brother."

Esau shook his head. "I have no need of your animals. Keep them for your sons, my brother."

Jacob bowed low. "Do not be angry with your servant. Take from my hand this offering as from a lesser to a greater."

Kneeling at his brother's feet, the man waited. I watched Esau's face as he chose peace. "Rise Jacob, my brother, I will accept your gift. We shall travel together to Seir, so that you may meet my family."

The men embraced again. Rachel smiled happily, still standing next to Jacob. Stepping back to bow again, my husband smiled and gestured widely to his family and the herds just topping the hill.

"Let not my brother be angry. We must travel slowly, for there are young animals in the flocks. Also, the children," he motioned again to his sturdy sons, "are young and weak. The women cannot travel long distances each day. We would only delay my lord as you return to your family."

"Then let me leave some of my men as guards and guides," Esau urged with a smile at his brother's description of his sons.

Another low bow with hand to forehead and heart. "Forgive me, my brother, what need have I of a guide? Is not this the land I have traveled through? Did I not herd sheep in these very hills? My own servants are protection enough to bring me to my father's tents." I forgot my exasperation with Jacob as I marveled at his smooth tongue. "Let us camp here together this night and make a feast to our kinship. In the morning we can part as brothers."

At Esau's nod, Jacob sent Asher and Issachar for a sheep and a goat from the flocks. The fires were laid. Bilhah helped Zilpah roasted the meat. Rachel and I kneaded bread and prepared vegetables. Reuben took seven of his brothers to the herds. As we worked, the boys and Jacob's servants drove the animals past the camp to the west, keeping to the high ground and moving slowly.

Later Simeon and Reuben sought me out. "Mother, why did Father honor Joseph above us, his oldest sons?" Their brother's name was spat out like an evil taste.

I was reminded of my own resentment as I put an arm around each broad shouldered son. I wasn't sure how to reply. "Rachel couldn't have children for so long," I started, feeling my way and trying not to fuel their hatred, "that your father believes Joseph is a blessing and a gift from God."

Simeon angrily twisted away from my touch. He stood staring at me, feet apart and hands clenched at his waist. "He is no more special than any of us." The enraged voice sounded loud and the deep tones startled me.

"Reuben is firstborn!" Simeon took up the argument. "Joseph has no right to special treatment!" Unlike his brother, his angry voice was low, hissing, and almost vicious. "Father is always giving Joseph honor above us all. He ignores you, too." The unexpected championing brought a lump to my throat.

I held out my hands in pleading to the two, angry young men. "Joseph is still young," I reminded them. "He will take his turn in the fields and with the flocks as he grows older. Perhaps Rachel will bear another child. Then Joseph will no longer be the special, only child."

"We'll see." Reuben sounded unconvinced. "Come, Simeon, we are needed with the flocks this night. The animals are to be moved on to the south before dawn."

"I will talk to your father when we are settled," I promised.

Both sons bent to kiss my cheek before they headed out to assist with the herding. I was left staring into the darkness and listening to the raucous celebration. Jacob was oblivious to his oldest sons' bitterness.

With jealous anger in my own heart, I wondered how I could make him see the danger. "God of my husband, why is he so blind?" I whispered into the night breezes. There was no reply and no ease to the hurt in my soul.

# Chapter 11

Travel in gradual stages brought us to the city of Shechem in the land of the Hivites. In comparison to Haran, the place barely rated being called a town. There were only a few mud houses sheltered against a hillside.

"The grazing is good here," Jacob announced. "I have bought this land for our tents. The men of this city are friendly. This is a good place for my sons to live."

So it was that we set-up a home outside Shechem. One of Jacob's first tasks was to erect an altar to his God. Using large stones hauled from the upper heights, he built an altar. When the men of the town asked what gods he honored, he replied "*El Elohe Israel*, the One God, the God of Israel." I was reminded of the night at Jabok when he was renamed Israel. He had never spoken of that night to anyone else and the memory gave me a warm feeling.

The elders honored my husband for his wealth and the stories of how the One God had blessed him. They never tired of hearing of Haran and how Laban had been duped by Jacob's God. Hamor, the chief of the town, told him, "It seems that your God is with you. We are honored that you have chosen to live with us."

One morning I confronted Jacob. "My lord, my husband, it is time for your youngest son to learn to work in the fields with his brothers. He is now nearly seven. All your other sons were shepherds at a much younger age."

Out of the corner of my eye, I saw Joseph standing in the shadow of Rachel's tent. She came to the doorway of the tent. The reply sent a spear of anger through me.

"Joseph is to have a tutor. Certainly you know that he is destined for a better future than a shepherd?" The question didn't require an answer as Jacob continued, "He must learn to read and write languages in order to fulfill his destiny. My son will learn to do figures and learn how to govern."

I saw Rachel lift her chin with a smug smile. Joseph tilted his head as though thinking, and then he, too, grinned in the shadows.

"I have sent to Haran for a learned man," Jacob continued.

"You set him apart from his brothers! You set your youngest above your eldest! How can you be so blind?" My voice was hoarse with emotion.

"He was born for greater things," Jacob tried to reason with me. I shook off the conciliatory hand.

"Your actions will bring only sorrow," I prophesied as I stormed away to sob alone in my tent.

The sight of Jacob and the tutor sitting with Joseph each day, not only fueled my anger, but provoked his brothers into harassing him. They delighted in tormenting the boy by leaving insects in his scrolls and nettles in his bed. Simeon was adept at thinking up new tricks to play on their brother. Young bodies honed by days running in the fields and climbing the hills easily defeated the scholar when he attempted retaliation. Laughing, even Zebulon, only a year older, held him off with one hand.

Eventually, he discovered that spouting some complicated fact caused his brothers to ignore him. I watched sadly as with each passing moon change he became more and more conceited. He even began to brag and strut about the camp. "My brothers, when I am a powerful Governor, I will not let you visit. You shall have none of my riches."

"You are tempting God," I warned more than once. "Your pride will be your downfall."

Both Rachel and Jacob laughed at my fears. "Leah, the boy is blessed by God," they insisted.

"Don't you act the same with your precious Dinah?" Leah challenged.

My one daughter was my joy. As she grew up she became more and more lovely. I never tired of combing and arranging her thick, soft, waist-length hair. The rhythm of the brush and the lustrous look and feel of her hair soothed me when my husband and sister frustrated me. For Dinah, I bought beautiful material from the passing traders and sewed elaborate gowns.

"Only the best and wisest of men will be your husband," I told her.

All around me, my sons were growing into young men. Before I really thought it possible, Reuben was nineteen. I knew that he and Simeon often went to the town to dance with the local girls at the festival dances. As often as I could I reminded them that the gods of Shechem were not the same as the One God of their father Jacob.

"Mother!" The tall, bearded man who was my oldest son laughed as he swung me around upon his return one evening. I smelled the strong beer from the feast on his breath. "Mother, of course the gods of Shechem aren't the God of my father. They are much more fun." And, with another drunken chuckle, "Besides, the women of Shechem offer themselves freely in honor of their gods on these festival days!" With another whirl, he set me down to stagger to his tent.

Dinah, too, was growing up. She lost the awkwardness of childhood and began to take on the graceful softness of a young woman. Sometimes she went to Shechem where she made friends with the local girls. With surprise, I realized that my youngest child was thirteen and a young woman. It was time to think about a husband for her. Jacob was not pleased when I approached him to remind him of his duties.

"Your daughter is of an age when she should be wed," I told the father one evening.

Looking up from the scroll he was reviewing with Joseph, he frowned, "Dinah is but a child."

"No longer." I shook my head, gesturing to where she stood with her brothers. The light of the moon illuminated the scene. The unmistakably feminine form was plain to see even in the simple tunic she wore. Her hair was neatly braided, and with each move, she expressed the grace of a woman. "It is time to celebrate her becoming a woman."

With a sigh, the father bent his head. "Very well, see to the preparations," he responded finally.

"You will seek out a groom for your daughter?" I pressed.

"There is time enough," he growled. "Leave me now," he added at the moment I would have spoken again.

In the morning I sought out my sister, as well as Bilhah and Zilpah. "Dinah is now a woman," I announced. "We must prepare to celebrate the event." With mixed feelings, I worked beside the women making the foods for the ritual that announced to the world that my daughter was a woman, ready to be a bride.

In the light of the full moon, she was bathed and dressed in a new tunic. Her hair was braided with beads and ribbons, then the new linen gown was dropped over her head. Proudly, Jacob led her through the camp. Inwardly, I mourned the fact that there could be no litter carried through the streets of Haran. The noble guests from the town included Hamor, the chief, and his son, Shechem. The high priests of the local temple also attended; however, they frowned when Jacob prayed for blessings on his daughter.

"God of Abraham and Isaac, make this your daughter a blessing to her family. Make this woman wise and give her many sons to teach in your ways. May she be a fruitful vine to her husband and raise up descendants to your glory." With the prayer finished, he kissed her on the forehead.

The celebration lasted until the morning light touched the horizon. Drunken and exhausted, the men of Shechem wandered to their homes.

It was not long after that she came to me with the request I had been half-dreading and half expecting. "There is a festival tonight," Dinah told me one morning. "Mother, say that I can go and join with the other girls in the dance. I could wear my new linen gown and the shawl you just finished."

"Why would you want to dance at a feast honoring other gods?" I hoped my question would dissuade her. I hated to refuse the eager look in her eyes.

With a laugh, she bent and kissed me, "Dear Mother, you know I honor only the One God. I just want to go and have fun with my friends." Still, I shook my head until she pouted and said, "Father will let me go."

With great misgivings, I gave in to her pleading. I couldn't sleep hearing the drumming and music from Shechem. But, I heard the muffled weeping when she returned. In a moment I had her in my arms inside my tent. The torn dress, tangled hair, and wrenching sobs told me all I needed to know. I pressed the back of my hand against my mouth to prevent a wail from erupting. Nothing could be gained by adding my anguish to hers.

"Hush, my dear," I rocked and comforted the girl until dawn. Finally, she slept and then I sought Jacob where he sat with the servant men, contentedly munching the morning flatbread.

"Come with me." The tone of voice brought him to his feet. Perhaps he saw the anguish in my eyes. Without question he followed me. At the entrance to my tent I told him, "Dinah went to the festival last night."

He nodded, "She wanted to be with her friends."

"Shechem, son of Hamor, chief of this place, has defiled your daughter." I stated the truth harshly, only barely preventing myself from screaming. "Dinah was raped last night."

The man staggered and held onto the tent pole. With the other hand he covered his face. A low moan came from his lips. "No, this cannot be. My sweet Dinah." His words of grief echoed the cry in my mind. For a long time, he stood with head and shoulders bowed. At last, he straightened. "I will send for her brothers. When they come in from the fields, we will deal with this." He strode away and a few minutes later a small boy ran toward the flocks to summon Reuben, Simeon, and the rest of the sons of Jacob.

It was mid-morning when they arrived. I saw my husband meet them. The angry roar that greeted the news was satisfying. I smiled grimly and returned to my daughter's side.

"You will be vindicated," I told the sleeping girl, brushing her hair gently with my hand. She continued to sleep, exhausted by her tears and frightening experience.

I returned to my post at the tent entrance just in time to see Hamor bow his way into Jacob's presence. My husband stood proud and angry with his sons arrayed behind him. Hamor groveled. He was pleading, but I could not hear for what. I saw Simeon clench his fist and step forward to be stopped by Reuben's hand. Jacob shook his head. Then I saw Levi speak. Hamor looked startled and shook his head. My husband turned as if to end the conference. The chief of Shechem held up a hand. I saw him shrug as he spoke. Then he bowed from the camp.

Unable to restrain my curiosity, I ran to Jacob while he still stared after the departing man. "My husband," I said as I grabbed his arm. "Tell me."

"It seems that Shechem wants to marry our Dinah." A terrible smile touched his face.

"After what he did to her?" I was astounded. "You would not consider such a thing?"

"Not unless he agrees to circumcision!" Levi smiled grimly.

Openmouthed, I stared at my son. Then I laughed. "He would not do such a thing!"

My sons nodded and Simeon added, "He would not dare show his face in the town and agree to such a thing."

They were wrong. Shechem himself came to the camp with Hamor. Jacob greeted the men gravely and they entered his tent.

Judah came to me. "Hear what Hamor has said." The words gritted out past angrily compressed lips. "He told my father, 'My son, Shechem finds the daughter of Jacob bar Isaac so lovely and desirable that no sacrifice is too great. With joy, he offers to be first to submit to this ritual.' " He paused for breath and continued. "They also promise that all the men of the town will submit to circumcision."

I was stunned into silence, but at his next words I found my voice. "Dinah is to come now and go with Shechem. Father is performing the act now."

"How can he give his daughter to such a man?" I sputtered in rage. "A man who would shame her so before her family and God!"

Judah put his hand on my arm, "Mother, trust me, Dinah will not be shamed."

I looked into his eyes and saw a purpose beyond his sixteen years.

"Tell your father Dinah will await her husband here." I turned to tell Dinah and prepare her for going with the man.

I stood with my arm around my daughter's shoulder. Rachel and the maids joined me. Dressed in a new gown with beads in her hair and necklaces at her throat, I was proud of the woman who stood where yesterday a child danced.

"You will be avenged, my child," I whispered to her.

She shuddered as a yip of pain drifted to our ears. "Father asks too much," she replied in a low tone. I wasn't sure if she meant he asked too much of her or of Shechem.

"Your innocence will be avenged," I repeated. "Neither your father nor your brothers will let such an insult go unpunished."

"Will I indeed be wed to Shechem, son of Hamor?" she asked. Her eyes were wide with something I couldn't identify.

"Would that be bad?" Her aunt looked at her with surprise.

"Yes ... no ... I ... he forced me." Dinah stumbled over the words. "He had no right to do that." Proudly she lifted her chin. "I am not one of the town girls who lays with any man at the festival."

Silenced, Rachel looked at her niece. After a minute, the girl continued more softly. "He has sought to make it right by marriage. He even allowed this ritual." Thoughtfully, she looked toward the tent where her brothers stood in silence.

"So," my sister probed, unable to leave the subject, "will it be so bad to marry Shechem?"

Dinah stared at the woman. "I could never forget what he did," she spoke coldly.

Further conversation was impossible, for the tent flap of Jacob's tent lifted. Hamor and his son staggered into the sunlight.

Heartily, Jacob's voice rang out, "Come, greet your bride."

I hastily dropped the veil over Dinah's frowning face. I gripped her hand and whispered. "Trust your brothers."

"Dinah, my daughter," Jacob kissed her and took her hand. "From this day you will be the wife of Shechem, son of

Hamor the Hivite, of the town of Shechem. May you be blessed with many sons. I pray the God of Abraham and Isaac will open your womb and make you fruitful." He placed her hand in Shechem's.

Hamor announced, "A feast will be given to celebrate this day. The house of Jacob bar Isaac has been joined to the house of Hamor, chief of Shechem."

Jacob turned and reminded the man, "A bargain must be kept first. Payment must be made."

"Tomorrow."

With many kisses, Dinah's brothers let her go. I saw that their faces could barely mask the fury.

A tent was set up near the city gate. Jacob waited with Reuben, Simeon, Levi and Judah for the men of Shechem to arrive. Hamor encouraged his friends with promises of wives and riches to be gained by agreeing to the circumcision. The men entered slowly, only to limp out a few minutes later.

Silently, Bilhah and Zilpah helped me prepare for the anticipated wedding banquet that was to be held in a week. My heart ached for Dinah. I had not seen her since she was led away between Shechem and Hamor. My daughter had walked proudly and I comforted myself by remembering the promise of Levi and Simeon.

"Mother, our sister shall be avenged. We have a plan." I dared not ask any questions, for I feared the cold rage I saw in their eyes.

Three days passed. All of the men of Shechem had come to Jacob's tent. No one from the camp of Jacob entered the town. It felt more like a time of mourning than of preparation for a celebration. Early on the third morning, Simeon and Levi slipped from their tents. By the time the sun rose, Hamor and his son were dead. Dinah was in my arms. Then all Jacob's sons ravaged the town. The smell of burning wood and flesh awakened anyone who slept past sunrise. I was appalled when the women and children were herded into the camp. Through tears and moans, they told of the early morning attack that left them widows and orphans.

"You will be taken care of," I promised. Zilpah hurried to gather all of the servant women to erect another tent. Bilhah found blankets. Dinah brought water and tried to comfort her friends. Together we settled the frightened women into the shelter.

Jacob greeted his sons with anger, but I knew that underneath the bluster was pride. His rage was to impress the visiting trader from Damascus. Word would travel through Canaan and beyond of my sons' defense of their sister Dinah.

"My sons, what have you done?" He confronted them as they strode up the hill after the fleeing women. Their hands still held bloodied swords and their tunics were covered with soot and blood. "You have made me into a traitor and liar. Nearby towns will hear of your deceitful actions. We will be driven away from this place."

"Would you have us ignore our sister's shame?" Reuben stood face to face with his father. I noticed with surprise that he was now taller than Jacob. "None of our women would be safe from such ruin if this action had not been taken. Didn't you hear Hamor promising our women as brides and all your wealth to the men of Shechem?"

"Dinah's shame had to be avenged," stated Simeon, standing next to his brother. His broad shoulders and height made him an intimidating figure.

Jacob's other eight sons murmured in agreement. I saw that Joseph was not among the brothers. Curious, I looked around to see Rachel holding tightly to his hand. For once he looked mutinous about being kept from his brothers activities. I could see him arguing with his mother. Finally, he jerked his hand free and stormed off toward the hills.

"The men of Shechem would never have honored Dinah in a way befitting the daughter of Jacob," inserted Levi. "Our sister is not a prostitute."

"We have avenged her honor," Judah shouted, raising a fist in the air.

Shoulder to shoulder the boys turned into men before my eyes. I wanted to cheer and hug them, but I didn't dare do either. Instead, I slipped away to deal with the hysterical women.

Rachel and I sat with Dinah that evening after everyone was fed. They were put to bed in the hastily erected tents with pillows and blankets brought in some cases from the devastated town. I was exhausted from the rushing and emotion of the day. Dinah leaned against my shoulder. Her words addressed my thoughts.

"I am glad to be here," she stated, as though making a decision. Then she added sadly, "But my friends are made widows and homeless. What will Father do now?"

From the shadows beyond the tent flap her father answered. "Those who have no family to return to will remain with us. Let it not be said that Jacob bar Isaac takes vengeance on women and children." His voice sounded weary and he walked slowly into the tent.

Rachel ran into his arms. "It was not you," she whispered loudly enough for me to hear. "Leah's sons took matters into their own hands."

I bristled at her words, but Dinah restrained me from answering sharply. The man kissed Rachel on the forehead. "They are also my sons, dearest love," he reminded her.

"Never mind. Come, rest, and forget." She pressed against him. With kiss and touch she led him from my tent to hers.

"Come, my mother," Dinah's words recalled me from my sad thoughts.

Once again Jacob chose Rachel for comfort. I replayed his defense of our sons trying to hear love and not condemnation. All I heard was pride in their manliness. Dinah urged me to my bed. Exhausted, I slept. But, my dreams were troubled by the memories of the women's tears and words.

# Chapter 12

Within a week, Jacob announced that it was time to go to Bethel. "My wives, the One God who met me on my way to Haran has come to me. It is time to fulfill the vow I made to Him then." He stood still and his eyes took on the faraway look I associated with his memories of that vision.

"We are ready," I answered, inwardly sighing as I thought of the travel and work now increased by the many women of Shechem. So many of them were under the protection of my husband.

Early in the morning Jacob called the entire camp together. Standing on a small hill he addressed everyone. "We will journey to Bethel, the place where the God of my father Isaac first met me. My God has told me that he will meet me there again."

Murmurs from the women of Shechem greeted his words. He seemed to ignore them, but I smiled to myself at his masterful winning of their loyalty. A man who could speak to the gods was a great chief to follow. "I was an arrogant young man who tricked my brother and stole his first-born's blessing." The words slid from his tongue as he told the story. His audience was in thrall as he continued. "With the excuse of seeking a wife from her kin, my mother sent me away from Esau's wrath. At Bethel I made my camp. That night I dreamed of a ladder reaching to heaven. The angels of God moved up and down the ladder." His eyes and face glowed with the memory. "The God of my fathers, the God of Abraham and Isaac, spoke to me. He promised to bring me safely back from my travels. To me he renewed the covenant made with my grandfather Abraham when He promised me descendants as the sand."

The man paused in his recital. No one moved. Even the children were silent, caught up in the awe of the adults. "I swore an oath to the God of my fathers that night. I pledged that if God would be with me to prosper my journey and give me family and wealth, I would return to worship Him at Bethel. I vowed to give him a tenth of all I gained." Whispers filled the pause as my husband looked around at the gathered people. Jacob's next words contained a command. "The God of Abraham and Isaac has been with me. He has blessed me with children and wives, with servants and flocks. He has given me widows and orphans to care for. The God of my fathers is not a bloodthirsty God, but He is a God who desires faithfulness. Therefore, put away all the other gods you have trusted in. The God I worship is the One God, the True God who made the heavens and the earth. He is the God who has made me rich and blessed me with my sons." His eyes sought the ten young men who stood together. He nodded at them. Then with a smile at his youngest son, he added, "God opened the womb of the barren to give me a precious gift and further blessing."

I had to grit my teeth against the angry words and scalding tears that boiled inside me. To have singled out Joseph, yet again, was unnecessary. I saw the frown on Levi's face and Judah's clenched fist as they glared at their half-brother. From the corner of my eye, I saw Rachel smirk as she smoothed her son's hair with her hand.

"The Lord has kept me safe in my travels and triumphed over those who would cheat me." Jacob then ordered, "At sunrise, bring all the gods and anything that is dedicated to an idol. We will bury them beneath the oak by the city. Then, with pure hearts, we can proceed and worship at Bethel."

I wondered if Rachel still had Laban's household gods and how she would explain their presence. I should not have worried. That night Joseph came to the fire as Jacob relaxed. In his hands was a bundle I recognized. I last saw it in Rachel's hands before we left Haran.

"My father, here are some strange figures I found in the bottom of a crate that broke open." His words were innocent as he handed the collection to Jacob.

The man unrolled the rug. His eyes lifted to meet mine and then shifted to Rachel. She reclined with eyes closed, resting after the excitement of the day's packing. I knew the memory of Laban's accusation was in his mind. My husband looked at Joseph.

"My son, God has brought these to light so that no abomination shall be hidden. We will bury these with all the gods of Shechem in the morning." Changing the subject he patted the mat he sat on. "My son, tell me of your studies."

The young man crouched beside his father. "Today I worked on the Egyptian. That is a hard thing to learn." He took a deep breath. "May I not skip these lessons? I will have no need of such skills."

"No, Joseph." Jacob shook his head. "You do not know what languages an official may have need of. In a few years, you will go to your grandfather in Haran. He will help you find a position with the *Gal* there or perhaps even the *LuGal* of the province. All your languages will be needed. Your knowledge will give you advantages over all the others. You will advance until you serve the king himself." A grand sweep of his hand helped paint the glorious picture of the favorite son's future.

"Father," the boy started to argue, "can't I spend time with the flocks?"

"Joseph," Rachel spoke up, "you make me proud with your studies. Your grandfather, too, will be honored by the position you will attain."

Sadly, he bowed his head and I saw the young shoulders move in a sigh. "Very well." His voice was low. Slowly he walked off into the darkness.

I felt a twinge of sympathy. "He is lonely," I remarked. "Would it be so bad for him to spend time with his brothers?"

Jacob shook his head. "My sons bear an honorable heritage as shepherds and chiefs of their families. I am a shepherd as were my father and Abraham the Wanderer before me." Proudly my husband lifted his head and his voice boomed into the night. "Joseph, however, is set apart for great things and I will not have him distracted." I shook my head at the stubborn insistence on learning. As an afterthought, Jacob added, "When he has learned the Egyptian as well as he knows the Sumerian, perhaps he can spend some time in the fields with his brothers. I will think about it after we are settled again. This time of travel is not a good time to learn to herd the animals."

Rachel snuggled close to her husband. I saw her hands reach up to stroke his face and he bent to kiss her. With sadness, I wandered to my tent. For a long time I sat staring at the night sky, listening to the murmur of my husband's many dependents settling for the night. The occasional bleat or low from the resting flocks drifted to my ears. My mind was busy contrasting my sons and their heritage with the plans for Joseph.

The morning dawned clear. The many wooden and stone figures of the gods of Shechem and Haran were buried beneath the oak that guarded the burnt gates of the city. It was the first time I had been close to the town since the rampage of destruction wrought by my sons. I felt sorry for the women who were looking for the last time on their destroyed homes. A few sobs were heard. Reuben and Simeon stepped close to two of the young women to offer comfort. Even Levi and Dan, as well as the two sixteen-year olds, Napthali and Gad, singled out girls to care for. When the girls didn't shun my sons, I knew that soon there would be weddings. Of course, they were not the first of my sons to wed, I mused, watching the young men with the girls. Judah had run away a year before. His anger with his father and brothers took him west to stay with his friend Hirah. When he returned from Adullam, he was married to a Canaanite girl named Darah. She was the daughter of a man named Shua from Timnah. A lovely and gentle girl, she now stood beside him holding my first grandson, Er. Judah had confided in me that she was again pregnant. Like all the people in the gathering, she hung on my husband's words.

Jacob announced, "We will start for Bethel when the moon is new, in a week."

Already my mind was making plans for packing and loading the camels and donkeys. I didn't know how far it was to this place my husband called Bethel, and the women of Shechem said was named Luz, but I wasn't looking forward to the trip. We set out one bright spring morning. Jacob and his sons, even Joseph, spent the night of the new moon in prayer at the altar. When dawn lit the eastern sky, they returned from the hill. The flocks were already starting out as we dismantled the tents and mounted the camels. Within a few miles, the dust from our travel obliterated any sight of Shechem behind us.

Jacob set a slow, but steady pace. "I will not seem to be fleeing," he said after the first day of travel. "Our gradual travel with the herds will make it clear that we are not planning any attacks."

Truly, we took our time. Men came from the surrounding areas to honor my husband as a great chief. They brought gifts, and many times we stopped after only a short distance to accept the offerings from some small local hill chief.

"The fear of Jacob's God is protecting us," I told Rachel. "They have seen how he is protected from danger and retaliation. All people see how God blesses our husband."

Rachel nodded, only half listening, as she lay back in the camel's saddle. "I wish we would stop moving," she whimpered, gagging suddenly.

"Are you pregnant?" I asked, the little hints suddenly making sense. Her listlessness, nausea, and refusal of certain foods could mean only one thing. She responded to my question with a nod and a wan smile.

"Have you told Jacob?" My words had a jealous edge. A second son for beloved Rachel, what would that mean for my sons?

"I will tell him soon," she replied, leaning back and closing her eyes.

My own eyes stared straight ahead not seeing the changing terrain but remembering the glowing face of my husband when Joseph was born.

I knew Rachel told Jacob her news because he became even more solicitous of her comfort. Her camel led the way so the dust did not trouble her. Of course, Joseph and his tutor rode beside her. Another couple of days of slow travel and we reached Shiloh. Here we stayed two full days with great feasting and dancing.

Levi came to me before we left. I stood staring at the stars thinking again of the promise the One God made to Abraham and Isaac that was being fulfilled in Jacob. My hands absently rubbed the small of my back, aching from the day's work.

"Mother, you are tired." The concern in his voice touched me deeply.

"It is nothing," I assured him, arching my back in one last stretch. "I am much refreshed standing here looking at the stars."

"At least you are free from the camel and donkey dust kicked up by Joseph and his mother." The tone was hostile.

I put my hand on his cheek. A cheek that not so long ago was smooth and boyish. Now it was covered with a thickening beard. "My son, Rachel is pregnant. The travel and dust are making her sick," I explained.

"Then you should ride beside her and let Joseph eat dust," he snarled, not mollified.

"Levi, try not to judge your brother harshly. He obeys his father by remaining at his studies. I have heard him beg to be allowed to join you all with the flocks. Your father wants him to learn all he can." I stopped because my son jerked away from me.

"It would be better if he didn't come at all!" I was taken aback by the man's rage. "His lack of skill would frighten the animals. We don't have time to baby-sit a spoiled brat who wants to play at being a shepherd!"

"Levi," I said his name softly, trying to penetrate the anger. I couldn't see his face in the night but his words frightened me.

"You should ride in front out of the dust," he repeated, ignoring the hand I held out.

"We'll see," I replied.

"Yes, we will see!" His grim words drifted to me as he stamped away.

I never asked how it was arranged that my camel paced beside Rachel's while Joseph and his tutor rode behind in the dust. The last half of the journey to Bethel was easier because of my son's thoughtfulness. Still, I was glad to reach the

shrine at the town that all in Canaan called Luz. The elders
and priests of the town came out to meet Jacob.

"I come in peace," he assured them. "The God of my
father Isaac has called me to meet him here where I made a
vow many years ago."

Their welcome echoed words spoken many times on the
trek from Shechem south to Bethel. "Jacob, son of Isaac of
Canaan, we have heard that the God of your fathers has been
with you. The One God you call on has made you strong and
wealthy. It has been told how your God slays your enemies
and turns their treachery to your benefit."

Another of the elders took up the speech, "We see that the
stories are true. You stand before our gates, Jacob, grandson
of Abraham the Blessed of God. With our own eyes we see
your wealth and your large family. On our hills, we see your
flocks and herds. Your camp is a city unto itself and your kin
a nation."

A third man continued, "May the Lord your God bless
your pilgrimage to our humble town. May your presence be a
blessing to us."

Jacob bowed to the ground, prostrating himself before the
elders of Luz. "Your welcome is greater than I deserve. With
only my shepherd's staff, I passed the night here once long
ago. Because of my vision, I have called this place *Bethel*, the
house of God. Now, indeed the God of my Fathers has
blessed me as he promised. I come to offer a tenth of all I
own in thanksgiving to the One God." Standing, the man
held out his hands, palm up toward the elders of the town.
"My lords, when I came to you before, I had nothing. Now I
will give to you gifts from the richness God has given me that
you may be blessed in your hospitality." His hand swept in a
circle to indicate the animals and people he had. "Sanctify
yourselves," he invited, "and come to the sacrifice at the
moon's rising."

"We will," they responded.

True to his word, my husband sent Gad and Asher with sheep, goats, and camels bearing skins of wine to the leaders of Luz. He spent the week preparing an altar. I never saw him so particular. Even Joseph was pressed into service to find the smoothest stones. From far and wide his sons brought rock for the altar. Most he rejected but some he used. Slowly the shrine took shape around the stone he pointed out as the pillow on which he dreamed of the angel's ladder and God's blessing.

Each night he kept vigil at the altar in prayer to God. At last the final stone was laid. The tithe offering of perfect animals was separated from the herd.

"Everything is ready in the camp," I told him. "Come and rest before the evening."

"No," the man replied and shook his head. His eyes were glowing feverishly with zeal for his God. "I must stay here and pray that God will accept my offering this night." He stopped and stared at the altar. The wood was in order. The fire smoldered in the pot ready to light the sacrifice.

"How could your God refuse?" I asked, gesturing to the myriad animals milling in the pens beyond the altar. "Surely the God who has so blessed you will accept your offering of thanks."

"I have too often followed my own desires and listened to the council of men, not God." He bowed his head and I saw tears of remorse.

"Jacob, my husband, the God of your Fathers came to you here and promised you family and wealth. How can you doubt? Look at your camp and your flocks. Know that your God is faithful."

I put my hand on his arm. He took it in both his hands, and bending his head, kissed my palm. "Leah, my wife," he said as he looked at me, "Leah of the lovely eyes and the deep faith, you remind me of God's love each time I forget and begin to be afraid." With a kiss on my forehead, he added, "I sought a word of approval from God. He has sent you to remind me that he has blessed my journey."

We stood silent for several minutes. I treasured his words almost as much as if he had spoken of love. The sun began its descent.

"Come, we must get all my sons," he announced. "They will stand with me as I dedicate myself and them to the One God of Abraham and Isaac."

Hand in hand we entered the camp to call everyone to the sacrifice. Proudly, I saw Reuben take his stand on Jacob's right hand. Even Joseph's presence at his left didn't anger me. From Simeon to Zebulon, the other nine sons stood in order behind their father. In front, at the right of the altar, Zilpah stood beside me while Bilhah crouched near Rachel's pallet. My sister was still weak from the travel. She was gently carried from her tent to watch the ceremony. The elders of Luz gathered at the left of the table of sacrifice. Townsfolk, the women from Shechem and the rest of Jacob's servants mingled together in the low area in front of the altar.

Silence fell over the group when Jacob raised a lamb over his head while Reuben blew the ram's horn. The sacrifice began. A lamb for each son was placed on the altar with a prayer of dedication. Not surprisingly, Jacob's prayer for Joseph included praise for his special birth and for God's blessings on his extraordinary talents. I saw his brothers exchange glances. Jacob, in his religious ecstasy, didn't even notice as he sprinkled each of the young men with some of the blood to symbolize cleansing.

As the night drew on, I heard muffled snores in the crowd. Suddenly, one of the elders of the city stepped forward to face Jacob across the altar. A stir ran through the assemblage. "Jacob, son of Isaac, your God has spoken to me." My husband paused in his prayers and sacrifices. "Jacob bar Isaac, of blessed Abraham's lineage, your God has spoken." The flint knife dropped from his hand as Jacob fell to his knees when the old man continued. "You will no longer be called Jacob, the Deceiver. Your name will be Israel. You will be known as the one who strives with God and lives!" The voice boomed across the gathering, awakening anyone who dozed.

I clasped my hands together, remembering that night at the Jabok when God gave my husband the new name of Israel. Now, in the presence of all the tribe and the people of Luz, the name was confirmed.

"The Lord your God says, 'I will bless my son, Israel. Your descendants will become nations and kings. Your name will be remembered forever.' " With a low bow, the man stepped back from the altar.

From behind me, I heard a tambourine. It was Dinah in a song of praise as she danced forward. "Blessed be the God of Israel. Great and Mighty is his Name. With great love he blesses Israel, my father. He will bless all the children of his servant and make them great. Praise to the God of Israel."

My daughter whirled before the altar in a dance of celebration. I found my hands clapping in rhythm and wished I dared join her as several of the young women of Bethel and Shechem did. Their beauty and songs held the crowd spellbound until they ended with arms upraised in praise to God. Jacob rose from his knees. I saw his face in the fire on the altar. Once again he had felt the hand of God touch him. He took a flask of perfumed oil from Joseph that he poured over the whole altar. The sweet smell rose in the smoke and floated among all the people.

My husband stood in the cloud of incense and proclaimed, "Glory and honor to the God of Israel. This place shall be known as *El Bethel Israel.* This is the house of the God of Israel."

The sacrifices and feasting continued for a full week. The men of Bethel gave gifts to Jacob. They now called my husband 'Israel'. When he announced that we would travel on to Hebron to see Isaac, the entire town came out to bid us farewell and seek his blessing.

"Remember," my husband told the elders, "this city is blessed by the One True God as a place where he meets his people. It shall be a sanctuary for the children of Israel for all time."

I was amazed at the number of animals Jacob left with the priests at Luz for future offerings.

"Sacrifice at each new moon," he instructed the elders, "that the favor of the God of Israel continues in this place."

# Chapter 13

We took up our journey. Jacob was anxious to see his father at Hebron. Steadily, we moved south. As we neared Ephrath, Rachel began to cry and moan. I pulled my camel near to hers.

"Rachel, sister, what is it?"

"The baby!" she gasped. Her face was contorted in agony.

"Joseph," I called, "hurry to your father. Tell him we must stop, Rachel's time has come." I stretched my hand to take hers. She clung to me crying out with each plodding step the camel took. Even when I drew the animals to a stop and made them kneel, she continued to moan.

"Here, we will stop here and make camp." Jacob's orders were rapidly obeyed. Still he shouted, "Hurry, you fools, set up a tent for my Rachel."

When he lifted her from the camel, I was shocked at her white drawn face.

"My love, all will be well." The man kissed her cheek. "Rejoice, my sweet Rachel, you will bear me another son."

I saw her try to smile but instead she cried out as another pain gripped her.

"Come." I led the way to the hastily erected tent. Bilhah and Zilpah were already preparing the bed. Jacob carried his beloved into the shelter and laid her down. He continued to hold her hand. "Go!" I pushed my husband from the tent. "This is woman's work. Don't be afraid." My words hid my own fear.

Zilpah's eyes were concerned as she drew me aside. "The baby is early and not in position."

"We must try to turn him," I said, placing my hands on my sister's distended belly and feeling for myself a hard head where it should not be.

Rachel cried out as we pressed and kneaded until the child shifted. Even then the labor was hard and long. I saw my sister failing before my eyes.

"Sister, you must fight and give your child life!" I held her face between my hands trying to force stamina into her weakening body.

She roused and whispered, "It is too hard. You are the strong one. It is easy for you. I cannot go on."

"Then take my strength." I gripped her hand. She weakly tried to grasp my fingers and a tear rolled down her cheek.

"I can't."

"Yes, my sister, you must!" My teeth clenched together tightly as I lifted her shoulders and held her in my lap. "My energy is yours now," I told her. "Bear down and I will be here."

A weak animal scream pierced the tent as together we birthed the baby. My hands helped push the child into the world.

Bilhah said, "It is a boy, my mistress."

Rachel lifted one hand to touch the tiny head but the effort was too much and her hand slipped down to hang limply.

"He will be Ben-oni, the son of my sorrow," she gasped. "For I leave him."

"No!" I shook her. "You must not say so." Still I signaled to Zilpah to get Jacob.

"Sister," the voice was so weak I had to bend close to hear her, "care for my son as your own."

"You will hold him on your knee." My bracing words were greeted with a weak smile.

"No, Leah, the gates of the Ningizzida, the Land of No Return, are open for me."

"Here is Jacob." Our eyes met as he read in them my fear. Appalled, he fell to his knees beside Rachel. "My love." A gentle hand brushed the sweaty hair from her face. "We have a son."

"Ben-oni," she whispered, trying to smile at her beloved.

"No, he shall be Benjamin, son of the promise, for there will not be sorrow."

Neither remembered my presence in the tent. I still held Rachel in my arms. Jacob pressed his forehead to hers.

"Beloved wife ... for me ... live," he begged.

Her hand tried to lift and then she relaxed on a breath. I knew she was gone. Jacob, too, sensed it.

"Rachel, Rachel!" The cry filled the air. He took her in his arms, rocking and crying. Only then did I truly understand how much he loved my sister. I gave him sons, but she gave him the joy and the love of life that I had never learned to share.

"My sister, I am sorry." The words came from my heart to her spirit. "I sought to steal Jacob's love by proving that I was a better woman. I wronged you. Forgive me from wherever you are."

I left my husband holding his beloved. Tears of sorrow and remorse blinded me and I stumbled at the doorway. It was Joseph who steadied me. I looked into his clear young eyes. My words came from a full heart. "I'm sorry."

He looked stricken and hurried into the tent. I heard his voice join Jacob's in lament.

In my words to Joseph I sought forgiveness from him; however, he never knew it. My sons gathered around me.

"Rachel died giving birth," I told them. Then I looked for the baby. Zilpah stood nearby.

"We will need fresh milk," I told the hovering men. Anxious to occupy themselves, they all headed for the flock.

"Find a clean cloth to dip in the milk until we can make a milk bladder for little Benjamin here." He fit in my arms just as every one of my children had. I was comforted in my grief to care for Rachel's son.

Jacob's anguish sobered his sons. I was glad to see them offering comfort, even to Joseph. After the time of mourning, we left Rachel buried at Ephrath. In the custom of Haran, I included her favorite possessions in the tomb. Jacob erected a pillar over the place and sanctified it to the One God.

Jacob seemed more anxious than ever to reach Hebron and his father Isaac. Our arrival was greeted with great feasting. The old man was happy to touch each grandson's face, although he was so blind that he could not see them at all. I was delighted to meet my father's sister. Even as an old woman, she had the same beauty of face and form that Rachel had been graced with. She remarked on the resemblance in Dinah also.

"In you, my child, I see myself again. Do not let these men waste your beauty on anything less than a prince."

"I shall never marry." My daughter sadly told her grandmother what happened with Shechem, son of Hamor.

The old woman held her granddaughter tight. "Men are so foolish. Their rages and desires cause nothing but desolation. Dreams of grandeur lead only to sorrow. Who am I to judge?" She sadly shook her head. "I myself caused a rift between my husband and his son, between my elder and my younger son." Then her lips curved into a smile. "Who can say what God has in store for you? I never thought to see my sons together again; but, see, there they are."

My eyes followed the direction of her finger. Indeed Jacob and Esau were greeting each other in front of the tent of Isaac.

"That is good," I replied, wondering if Rebekah knew that Jacob sent for his brother.

"My father is dying," he told me soon after we arrived. "I have given him joy of heart with my return and now he is ready to die." His voice was sad. "I have lost so much time to my foolish pride and fear."

"Do not condemn yourself, my husband." I tried to comfort his sorrow. "Has not your God turned all to good?"

Finally, he raised his head and nodded, "What you say is right. I must send for Esau. It is fitting that together we keep vigil at my father's side."

So, now the two men entered the tent. My heart breathed a prayer for their coming grief.

"I am blessed for my sons are at peace." Rebekah's statement interrupted my thoughts. "And you, my niece, God has truly blessed you with sons. Twelve strong boys."

"Only six are from my womb," I reminded my aunt.

"All are yours by God's will," she said. Then with a sigh, she added, "My son is not wise to set Joseph apart. I made that mistake with Jacob and it has taken these long years to bring reconciliation."

I would have answered had not the young man in question hurried toward us. "Father says to come quickly." He held out his arm to assist Rebekah.

Together we hurried to Isaac's tent. Jacob and Esau stood side by side. Rebekah dropped to her knees and caressed her beloved husband's face, while tears ran down her own. "Isaac, my love…" She tried to call him back, but with a sigh he was gone. The two men began the death wail. It was echoed throughout the camp.

Word spread that Isaac bar Abraham was dead. Men came from the surrounding areas to grieve and honor the passing of the great patriarch. Esau and Jacob buried their father in the cave at Mamre. They laid him beside Abraham and Sarah. Within a few months, Rebekah, too, lay in the tomb. She had no desire to live without Isaac. I missed the wise, faithful woman that, in a few short weeks, I had grown to love. It was her strength and determination that united the tribe, especially as Isaac grew older and more frail. Now she was gone, and I found myself stepping into her shoes. I hoped I could fulfill my duties as well as my aunt had. Esau and Jacob parted, allied by their sorrow. Esau returned to the land of Seir where he had a family and wealth with flocks of his own. Jacob set up his tents near Hebron for the grazing was good. Isaac's flocks merged with ours. I was glad for the extra servants to help with the camp, which had now doubled in size.

# Chapter 14

Reuben and Simeon took on the management of the herds for Jacob. He was bowed low with his triple grief. I was glad to see that he let Joseph join his brothers. Whether this was because he finally saw the danger in making him the special son or because he was simply too deeply lost in his grief to care, I was not sure. It was enough that the young man was almost accepted by his brothers when he set aside his pride and worked in the fields.

Joseph still spent the evenings with his tutor in his father's tent. He seemed to enjoy gossiping about his brothers to Jacob. One night he asked, "Father, is it a good thing to leave the flocks and go to the village for wine?"

"Why do you ask?" was the reply, as the man glanced at his son.

"Dan and Napthali often leave the animals with me. When they return, they have skins of wine to drink," the young man reported.

Jacob's brows drew together and he sought his sons. I heard the angry voice as he confronted them.

Joseph sighed as he looked after his father, "Now again, they will hate me."

Indeed venomous looks were directed at the young man that evening as we ate together. Rachel's oldest son pretended to neither see nor care about their hatred. He forgot his brothers' rage a week later. It was his seventeenth birthday. Against my advice, Jacob procured a fabulous prince's coat for his son. Simeon and Levi could barely contain their feelings when they saw the gift. Reuben turned his head to hide the look of jealousy and all the rest made somewhat civil remarks.

"Joseph, you will soon travel to your uncle Laban in Haran to seek a position in the government. God has chosen you for great things. Your learning has prepared you to take your place with the powerful." Jacob repeated the promise again.

The women and servants admired the handsome young man as he paced through the camp. Benjamin acted as a herald for his brother as he capered ahead of him.

"See what my big brother got for his birthday," the child called to everyone. His innocent joy made me smile even as the ten siblings stalked away to their day's work in the fields and with the flocks. For all his arrogance, Joseph was gentle and kind to his little brother. Patiently, he spent hours each night listening to the boy chatter about his day's adventures involving chasing the dogs and catching lizards. Watching him catch the child into his arms as he paraded around showing off his gift, I could almost forget my sons' hatred of the young man.

The next morning; however, Joseph proudly strutted from his tent. "Listen my brothers," he proclaimed, "last night I had a dream."

"What do we care?" snarled Asher, turning his back to snatch up a piece of bread.

"Keep it to yourself," added Levi.

He ignored their disinterest and shared the dream. "It is about us all. We were in the fields at the harvest. Each one of us had a sheaf of wheat. Suddenly, my sheaf stood up straight and tall and yours all fell flat on the ground around it." The proud toss of his head was not well received.

"Take your dream somewhere else." Judah clenched his fist in threat.

"You will not rule over us," Levi exclaimed, with anger mounting in his eyes.

"Then I had another dream." The young man ignored the undercurrent of fury around the fire.

"Tell us, my son," Jacob encouraged Joseph. Looking around at his older sons the man added, "Dreams come from the One God and can tell us important things."

Standing next to his father, Joseph smiled. "This dream was about all our natal stars." A slight stir of interest from his brothers reminded me that they remembered the importance of the stars in the rituals of Haran. Although sixteen years had passed, the eldest of the sons of Jacob could remember watching the ceremonies directed at Utu and An, gods of sun and heavens. The priests happily expounded on the various merits of the constellation that rose on the day of a person's birth. It was believed that everyone's destiny was written in the stars by the gods. "Your stars and the sun and moon gathered around my star and paid homage. They bowed low in obeisance. What can this mean but that I am indeed destined for great things?" Joseph lifted his head as though a crown already rested there.

Reuben leapt to his feet. "Foolish boy," he snarled. "What are these but dreams of grandeur fed by our father!"

"Do you plan to begin to lord it over us?" Simeon angrily thrust his fist close to Joseph's face.

The rest rose and stormed away from the fire with similar comments.

Even Jacob scolded his son. "Do you think that your mother and I will bow to you? You go too far with your boasting. My son, the blessing from God is not meant to be a tool to shame your family."

Crestfallen, the young man walked away to sit under a tree away from camp. For the first time, Jacob seemed truly angry at his favorite. "Who does the boy think he is to announce such a dream?" he demanded. I turned to see him standing beside me. He stared at his son with fury.

"Did you not say that dreams are from God?" I asked.

My husband shook his head. "Perhaps I have put such thoughts into his head. Was I wrong to keep him separate from his brothers and give the boy special tutoring?" The tortured question hung in the air. My mind reviewed the many times I had thought the same thing. Now I sought to offer comfort.

"You and Rachel did what you believed best for the lad." I paused wondering if now was the time to share my fears for his safety. Jacob still stared at his son. Joseph sat with his head on his knees under the tree. Gently I took Jacob's hand in mine. "You prepared him for what you believed God planned for him," I added, hoping to ease the look of anguish.

"Perhaps," he spoke in a low tone, "or perhaps it was what we desired for him."

"Jacob, my husband, let him go to Laban and learn if God will promote him as you dreamed." The suggestion seemed a way to get the young man away from his brother's seething rage.

"Like my mother, you think he would be safer away from his brothers." Startled, I looked at the man. With a half smile, he nodded, "Yes, she spoke to me and warned me of his brothers' jealousy."

He fell silent and then announced, "The next caravan headed north will take Joseph to Haran."

The young man was pleased when he heard the plan. I saw him daily watching for signs of a caravan.

One morning Jacob called his son. "Your brothers have gone to Dothan with the flocks. Go and see how they are doing."

"What if a caravan comes?" Joseph protested.

"There is no word of approaching traders," Jacob assured him. "You will be back in little more than a week. This way you will be able to bid your brothers farewell. Make peace with them before you leave," he urged. "Ask forgiveness for the impertinence of your youth."

Father and son argued before I heard Joseph finally yield. "I will go, but I will travel alone," the young man announced. "I can go much faster by myself."

"Very well." Jacob reluctantly agreed and watched his beloved son trot off on a donkey. The wonderful coat was bright in the sun.

"It will be good for him," Jacob told me, as much to convince himself as me.

I felt a shiver of fear watching the proud young man disappearing in the distance. "May the God of my husband preserve him in safety," I whispered to fend off the dread.

"He will be back soon," I told the concerned father each morning when his eyes scanned the road.

A fortnight passed and no figure appeared on the horizon. Another week and then another. Early one morning I bent over the fire to stir the coals to life. The pre-dawn moment before the camp arose was time I had all to myself. This morning a sound reached my ears. "Flocks?" I wondered, looking up and squinting to the north. In the dim light I saw my sons topping the rise. With my heart in my throat, I stood frozen.

Jacob burst from his tent. "Why do I hear the herds?"

Silently I shook my head. Together we watched ten men approach. Their father glanced at them and stared past looking for another son.

"Father," Reuben took Jacob's arm, "my father, I fear we have bad news." He guided the man to a low stool by the fire.

"Where is Joseph?" The words came out as a croak.

"We hoped he was here." Reuben and his brothers moved forward to stand close to their father.

"No," Jacob shook his head, "I sent him to see how you were. I told him to make peace with you before he left for Haran."

I saw Simeon and Levi exchange a quick glance as Reuben knelt before his father. "Then evil has indeed befallen him," the man sighed, "just as we feared."

"What?" The word was forced out as the man stared from son to son trying to comprehend.

Simeon held out a bundle. Reuben took it when Jacob sat frozen. "We found this." My second son's voice was rough with suppressed emotion. I was not sure if it was grief or anger.

"Isn't it Joseph's birthday coat?" inserted Judah, as the blood stained garment unrolled to lie on my husband's lap.

I saw Jacob jerk from the contact. Very slowly one hand moved to touch the soiled embroidery and examine the torn cloth. "Joseph, my son, what has happened to you?" His voice broke on a sob. "Surely a wild animal has killed you." He buried his face in the stained robe and began to wail.

As one, nine men took a step backward from the intense grief. Only Reuben remained kneeling beside his father. With an unreadable expression he looked at his brothers. I thought I saw accusation but couldn't be sure.

"I will go to him but my son will never come back to me," Jacob cried. "Rachel, my beloved, I have failed you! Our son is dead!"

The man rocked back and forth in agony. Around him, the camp assembled. The news was whispered from ear to ear. "Joseph has been killed by wild beasts on his way to see his brothers."

I forced my feet to move. Crouching beside my husband, I drew him into my arms as I would a hurt child. None of my sons would meet my eyes and fear gripped me.

"They have truly killed their brother and hidden his body." The thought made me shudder and hold the man more tightly.

"My husband, perhaps he is not dead, just injured and hiding in a cave," I suggested. "Send your sons and servants to search."

"No, he is dead. My son is lost to me forever. His coat, my gift to him, is torn and bloodied." He held it up for me to see. "Joseph, the gift from God to Rachel, has been killed by wild animals. I have failed. Nothing is left of my beloved." Great wrenching sobs racked the big man.

Finally, I persuaded him to enter his tent. Over the next week, Dinah and I took turns sitting beside the grief-stricken father. Benjamin, in his childish way, tried to comfort the man by snuggling into his arms. It was only with his youngest son that Jacob stopped moaning.

"My son, I will keep you safe," he promised the lad over and over. "You are all I have left of Rachel."

Hearing his words, the old flame of jealousy sprang to life in me again. "Do not forget you have ten other sons," I cautioned.

"They are grown men," he replied, "with families of their own. I must keep the boy safe for Rachel's sake."

I left my husband to the ministrations of my daughter and youngest son. They were finally able to coax their father from the depths of his grief. The day he emerged from the tent, a sigh of relief was heard in the camp. The man seemed much older. Anguish bowed the once straight, proud back, and I heard him beseeching God's forgiveness every time he prayed. Daily, he visited the altar erected by Abraham at Hebron.

"It is not your fault that Joseph went to see his brothers." I tried to console my husband. "You sent him to make peace. Surely that is a good thing."

"I was angry with his presumptuous dreams," Jacob finally confessed. "My last words to him were spoken in frustration and anger. I told him to make peace because he offended me by claiming the very thing I told him was his destiny." The graying head bowed into his hands. "Now the dream is gone. I was too proud and God has chastised me."

I had no words of comfort and could only rest my hand on his shoulder to offer sympathy. He did not want my solace and took to walking alone in the hills.

"He is seeking forgiveness from his God," I told Reuben. "Your father blames himself for Joseph's death."

"My mother." The man turned to me, a tormented expression in his eyes.

"Yes, my son?" I waited, but he shook his head. "You can tell me what troubles you," I whispered.

He shrugged, "It is nothing." After a moment of silence, he added, "We will keep a watch when Father is in the hills. He will not know we are near, but we will keep him safe."

I watched him walk away. His lack of trust frustrated me, and his obviously troubled heart worried me. It was years before I learned the truth.

# Chapter 15

The loss of Joseph aged Jacob overnight. He took no interest in the flocks and fields. The camp turned into a permanent tent city near Hebron. I was rather relieved that the endless traveling from camp to camp was ended. Still, I mourned over the sorrow of my husband.

"God of my husband," I challenged, "why have you done this to him? Is this not the same Jacob you promised wealth and honor to? If you are God, won't you help your servant." Angrily, I called to the silent stars in the night sky. "He believed in you and you have struck down his dreams. Who are you God, to withhold your favor and kill all those your servant loves? You called him Israel as a sign of your blessing. Where is that help now?" I heard no answer to my confrontation. My heart ached to ease Jacob's sorrow but he shut me out, too.

The men of Canaan soon learned to turn to Reuben and Levi for business matters. Judah and Simeon gradually took on more and more of the responsibility for the herds. They decided the time of shearing and located the best pastures.

The anniversary of Joseph's death arrived and Jacob spent the day alone at the altar on the hillside. A few weeks later, Gad approached me to say that he had found a girl he wanted to marry. Hannah was gentle and sweet. Even though she was from Hebron, she was willing to follow the One God of the family she joined. The wedding feast was full of joy. Jacob actually smiled at one of the jokes shared around the fire.

After the wedding week, Gad returned to the flocks and Hannah joined Dinah in encouraging her new father-in-law to join them on daily walks. One day I saw him returning with the young women, decked out in flower chains, but smiling and relaxed for the first time in over a year. I rushed to embrace my husband and he didn't rebuff me. That night we lay together in his tent. My love enfolded him and slowly the healing began. In the stillness of the night he began to talk about his mother and Joseph. I felt a closeness to my husband that I never experienced before.

"I never understood how hard it was for my mother to send me away," he remarked. The waning moon tried to peek into the tent as he talked. "I was her favorite. Esau was too rough for her. She dreamed for me the same dreams I wanted for Joseph." He drew a ragged sigh at his son's name. "God had other plans."

"She rejoiced when you returned," I reminded the man as he sat silent with bowed head. "You left with only your staff and came back the head of a nation. Your God blessed you above your brother."

His hand tightened on mine. "My wife, God has also taken from me my mother, my father, my beloved Rachel, and her son. I will never see them again."

The sorrow in his voice wrenched my heart. Briefly a thought flitted through my mind, questioning if he would miss me if I had died rather than Rachel. As if in answer he brought my hand to his lips. "Leah, promise you will not die and leave me desolate."

"My husband." My free hand caressed his bent head. Tears made it impossible for me to speak. We clung to each other in the darkness. I rejoiced, as I understood that he needed me even if he didn't love me as he still did my sister.

The next day he sent for his sons and requested a report of the flocks. Proudly, I looked at my tall, broad shouldered

sons as they spoke of pasture and profits. I missed that they
no longer sought me out for confidences. Dinah reminded
me that they were men with families of their own. Indeed, all
the men except Zebulon had found wives and were raising
promising families and flocks of their own. Still, I could not
rid myself of the feeling that they were all hiding something
from me.

Eight years passed in the same fashion. The spring births
of calves, lambs and kids were followed by the shearing time
and then the harvest festivals in the fall. Winter was a time of
gathering around the fires and telling the stories of Abraham
the Wanderer, Isaac, his son, and the blessings on Jacob. All
the neighboring chiefs called my husband Israel, but I still
preferred to call him Jacob. It reminded me of the young man
I first saw forty years earlier. Despite the fact that his hair was
now graying, I still loved him as much as I did then. I knew
that my own body too showed the signs of the years. My hair
was wirier than ever and it now showed more gray than black.
Never slender, I was now plump. The grandchildren loved to
come to see me because, like Laban, I kept a supply of
sweetmeats to hand out. All the women in the camp sought
my advice and I was present at each birth and death.

The eighth spring shearing passed and we prepared for the
wedding of my first-born grandson to a virgin from Timnah.
Her name was Tamar. I was impressed with her poise. For
one barely old enough to be a bride, she had the confidence
and bearing of an older woman. She faced her marriage to
fourteen year-old Er with composure, even though she had
never met him.

"Tamar, aren't you a little afraid?" Dinah asked as she
fastened another dowry chain around the slender neck. "I
remember ..." She stopped and shook her head.

"Of course," the girl replied, looking at my daughter with
her unusual amber eyes. Framed by long dark lashes, the calm

eyes were the first thing you noticed about Tamar. "I have no woman to tell me what to expect, but I have to trust that my father has chosen what is best for me."

Dinah smoothed the straight, lustrous black hair over the heavy jewelry and took the bridal headdress from me. Impulsively she hugged her soon to be sister. "It can be quite wonderful, I think, if you have the time to learn to love each other," she said glancing at me. "My mother and father have many years together and so many sons. I wish you the same joy."

The wedding week was followed all to soon by tragedy. Within a season, Er was dead. A fever claimed him. Even Zilpah's constant care and my skills with healing herbs could not save him. When the time of mourning was over, Judah brought his second son to me. "Mother, explain to Onan why he must marry Tamar."

There was a surly look on the boy's face, "I don't want Er's wife, I want my own."

"That may happen in time," I replied. "First, it is your duty to bless your brother's memory with a child so his line will not end."

"Any child born of my seed will be my flesh and bear my name," he stated shaking his head. I was surprised at such words from a thirteen-year old.

"You are standing in your brother's place," I explained, trying to be patient with the young man whose eyes narrowed more and more as I talked. "Just as I consider Gad and Asher my sons, although I did not physically bear them, the first child born to you and Tamar will be considered as Er's. It is the only way to ensure that Er's name does not disappear. A man's seed is sacred to God, as is his offspring. In doing this, you will honor your brother."

"I will not do it," he stated.

Judah caught his son by the shoulder when he started to stamp from the tent. "You will marry Tamar and the child will be your brother's." Two pairs of stubborn and angry eyes glared at each other. I was afraid Judah would strike the boy if he refused again. He was gripping his son's shoulders savagely in his combined grief and rage. "You will not dishonor your brother's life and memory by refusing to follow the tradition laid down long ago." When he was angry, Judah's voice became very low and I felt a chill as he continued to hold Onan's shoulders and glare at him.

"Very well." The young man jerked himself free and rushed out of the tent.

My son sank down with his head in his hands. "Did I do the right thing? Could God be punishing me?" In the anguish of his voice, I heard uncertainty as well as anger. "It is not fair that Er died. He was so young. His brother must give Tamar a child so his memory will not die."

Gently I smoothed back his hair. I would have taken him in my arms to offer comfort, but I knew that he would refuse me. So I said, "Onan, too, is grieving. I'm sure he will understand that you are right and provide a son for Er's memory."

My grandson did indeed marry Tamar. He spent little time with her, preferring to visit the shrines and prostitutes of the Canaanite gods with his friends. Judah's rebukes did little good. When forced to remember his duty, the young man spent time with his bride. We all waited expectantly for news of a child.

Late one afternoon, I saw Dinah walking with her sister-in-law. "Tamar, when will you make us all glad with news of a baby?" Dinah's words made me pause to hear the answer.

"I fear there will be no child any time." A lowered head accompanied the sad response.

"What do you mean?" questioned my daughter.

"Onan comes to my tent rarely; but, even when he does lie with me," she sighed, "he spills his seed on the ground."

Dinah took the woman in her arms as the tears started to flow. "My sister, I am so sorry."

"He has told me again and again that he will not give me a child because he hates his brother for dying."

I slipped away quietly as Dinah tried to comfort Tamar. Her words rang in my ears.

"God, please do not punish him for shaming his brother," I prayed.

The prayer was not answered; Onan fell from his donkey when returning home drunk after the harvest festival in Hebron. His head struck a rock. When Judah found him in the morning, he was dead.

My son was torn by grief and guilt. "If I had not forced him into marriage with Tamar, he would still be alive." The statement came from the man who sat with his head in his hands in my tent. "Er was taken from me to remind me ..." His voice trailed off. After a moment, he continued, "Onan chose to follow the ways of the locals rather than raise up a child for his brother. Shelah is my only hope for heirs."

"Onan already enjoyed the Canaanite ways before he married Tamar," I reminded Judah. "It was not being a husband that turned him from the One God. It was his own rebellion."

"Still, I will not give Shelah to Tamar now. He is too young. I will send her back to her father until he is older. How can I risk God's punishment on my youngest son?" He ran his hand through his hair making it stand on end. "Perhaps it is Tamar that is cursed." The man raised his head to look at me. He was looking for absolution and I was unable to give it to him.

I shook my head. "Tamar is not evil. The fever that took Er also claimed many others both young and old in the camp and in the town," I reminded him. "Onan fell from his donkey in a drunken stupor. That was his chosen lifestyle. Neither you or Tamar had anything to do with it."

My words fell on deaf ears. The young woman was sent away to her father in Timnah. Judah promised to send for her again when Shelah was old enough to be a true husband. Four years passed. The boy was fifteen and still Judah delayed. He did not send for Tamar.

The death of Judah's wife, Darah, gave him an excuse to again postpone the expected wedding. The spring shearing time came and he put off his mourning. "I am going with my friend Hirah to the shearing at Timnah," he announced one morning. Jacob sent him on his way with a blessing and a request for news.

"Bring Tamar back," I urged. "Shelah is old enough now and surely she will be expecting you to send for her."

The man did not respond. He trotted from the camp next to his friend without a backward glance.

"Will he bring Tamar?" Dinah asked as we stood together watching the two donkeys disappear into their own dust clouds as they headed west.

I shook my head. "I don't know, but I fear not. He is too concerned for Shelah's life."

Judah returned a month later without Tamar. "She can remain a widow in her father's house," he replied, thin lipped and angry when I confronted him. "I will not give Shelah to her. He would surely die. Perhaps I will wed again and raise more sons to provide heirs."

"My son, why do you hate her so?" He didn't answer my question, but turned and stamped away.

The rumors started at the next moon festival. I first heard it from Dinah. "The women in town are saying that Tamar is pregnant. She was seen by Judith and Marah at the feast."

"How?" The question was foolish but burst out anyway.

"Obviously, she is not as pure and faithful as her widow's garments would indicate," Zilpah chuckled. "Judah will not be pleased."

She was right. My son came raging into my tent. "Have you heard? Tamar is with child! How dare she play the whore? She will pay for this. Everyone knows that she is betrothed to Shelah, yet she shows her true colors now. I would have freed her to marry another if she asked!"

I let him rant and pace. Finally he sank down on the pillows, spent with emotion. "You know the punishment for such an act?" I asked.

"Yes." I tilted my head for he did not look sad at the idea of destroying the woman. "I have sent Abdul and two servants to bring her here to be burnt. Such impurity must be cleansed. She will not shame the name of Judah bar Jacob and his sons." The man clenched his fist and pounded it into the palm of his hand to emphasize the point.

"Will you not hear her story?" I asked.

"Why should I?" He raised his chin proudly. "She has publicly played me false. No one will prevent me from ridding myself of her evil."

"My son ..." He didn't let me finish.

"Mother, I will do what must be done."

We heard the commotion as Tamar was brought into camp. Jeers, hisses, and the dull thud of sticks on flesh drifted into the tent. Still Judah didn't go outside. "I will wait until the fire is ready. There is no need for me to be involved beyond lighting the wood," he stated turning his back on me when I held out my hand.

"My mistress." Zilpah stood at the tent opening. Beside her I saw Judah's servant, Abdul. He held something in his hand. Something was wrapped in a linen scarf. "The woman bade me give you these and said 'Tell my father-in-law that these belong to the man who made me pregnant.'"

"Thank you," I said when my son made no reply except to take the bundle. With a bow the two left and the tent flap dropped into place. "Now you will know the truth," I pointed out.

Judah was turning the packet over in his hands and fingering the scarf. "It could not be." His voice was hoarse. "There was a shrine prostitute at Enaim ..." Still he turned the bundle over and over. "I went in to her on the way to the shearing ..." Pleading eyes looked at me. "I had not had a woman since my wife, since Darah died." He looked down at the proof in his hands. One finger flicked the dangling fringe. "The woman wore a scarf like this." With shaking hands, he unrolled the material. We both stared in shock as a seal and staff fell onto the cushion and rolled to the dirt floor. Judah fell to his knees. He picked up the cylinder. The image on the seal proclaimed his sanction of treaties and ownership of property. I had seen him use it on the marriage document for Onan. "I gave these to the prostitute at the shrine as a sign that I would send a kid from the flock as payment. When Hirah took the offering he could not find the woman. This is proof of my guilt. I did not give Shelah to Tamar as I swore. She has provided herself with a son of my seed to preserve my lineage." The man was rocking back and forth in shame and regret.

"Then the woman is blameless." Jacob's voice startled me.

Judah stood up and faced his father. Bravely, he looked straight into the brown eyes that held sympathy rather than condemnation. "She is more righteous than me. I will take her into my household again. The woman was doing what she had to because I ..." He raked his fingers through his hair and confessed. "My oath was broken because of fear. I did not trust in your God, my father." With a groan, he lowered his head to look at the scarf he still held.

Judah squared his shoulders and pushed past his father. He lifted the tent flap and went out. We followed. His presence silenced the murmuring. Everyone held their breath in anticipation. The man strode decisively to where Tamar was bound. Her hands were tied and the woodpile was at her back. Her mourning clothes and head veil had been ripped away. The under-tunic barely covered her to the knees. Still, she stood with her head high watching him approach. The young woman did not flinch from his frown. Calmly she gazed at my son. In one hand, he held the staff and seal. With the other, he drew his knife. A gasp rose from the watchers. He sliced through the binding ropes. "Tamar, because I delayed to give you my son Shelah in marriage, you acted to preserve a heritage for me. It seems that you have earned the right to my protection." The man and woman looked at each other silently while the crowd held its breath. "Both you and the child of my seed, which you carry, will remain in my tents."

"My lord is generous and wise," Tamar demurely bowed her head. She did not move until Judah took her arm.

"Go," he growled, giving her a slight push. "In my tents you will have a home. I will not come to you again," he promised.

Dinah stepped forward. "Come my sister," she urged. Linking arms with Tamar she led her through the parting crowd. I gathered a newly woven blanket and hurried to join the young women. Draping the soft wool over her shoulders I walked beside the woman who would bear a son for Judah. The camp came alive with the buzz of excited whispers. Judah stood staring at the wood piled ready to burn the woman. Then he stalked up the hill to spend time alone with his thoughts.

The months slid by. Zilpah tended Tamar and told me she was sure that there were twins in the womb. The midwinter cold settled in the valleys and was barely kept at bay by fires and blankets. Dinah came for me before the sun rose one morning. "Mother, Tamar's time has come."

I roused Zilpah. The three of us scurried across the frosty ground to Tamar's small tent tucked safely next to Judah's. Tamar gasped as a pain caught her. Zilpah chuckled and remarked, "The little one has sent his hand to feel this new world." She tied red string to his wrist. "This will protect the firstborn from evil." We gasped as the hand disappeared. A head replaced the groping fingers. "Ah, now he is born." She smiled while Tamar panted, and the baby slid into the world. "But this is not the brave one." She held him up to show that his arm did not have the red string. His shrill cry broke the cold air and Zilpah handed him to Dinah to wash and wrap snugly. Tamar smiled when Zilpah remarked, "That one forced his way past his brother."

"He will be called Perez," the mother announced, "for he made a breach past his sibling."

Another spasm and the other baby boy greeted the cold morning with a wail. "Here is the questing one," Zilpah announced. "See the string I tied to his wrist?"

"Your name is Zerah because you reached for the light first." Tamar smiled at her twins when Dinah placed them in her arms. "My sons." Her face was soft and contented.

Zilpah and Dinah tended to Tamar. I went to find Judah, breathing a prayer of thanks. "God of my husband, your blessings are wonderful. I see how you have returned sons to my son." Judah was standing at the entrance to his tent. Haunted eyes were fixed on Tamar's tent. "You have fine healthy twin sons," I told him. "The God of Israel has given back that which you thought was lost. Tamar is safely delivered and has named the babies Zerah and Perez."

"The woman has survived?" he asked in a choked voice.

"Tamar will be a wonderful mother," I assured him. "Will you come and meet your sons?" I saw the struggle in his face. Desire to see his new sons warred with the guilt and shame he daily wrestled with. "Do not hold their conception against them." I touched his arm and looked up into his eyes. "God has blessed you with two strong sons."

"You are right." He nodded and turned to cross the short distance. At the entrance, he hesitated. I saw him raise his hand to lift the flap. It dropped back to his side. I pushed aside the leather door. My son took a deep breath before stepping into the tent.

"Tamar?" Her name was a question and a request for permission to enter.

"Judah, my lord, come and see your sons." She lay back on the mound of pillows. Warmly comfortable, she was nestled in blankets and skins with a tiny bundle on each arm. Slowly the man crossed the floor to kneel beside the woman. "This is Zerah," she introduced father and son, "because he reached out first before his brother Perez was born. See Zilpah put a red string on his wrist for protection when he stretched out his hand from the womb." She uncovered the little arm to show him.

"Then he is the firstborn." Judah smiled for the first time as the tiny fist flailed in the air. Gently he captured it and tucked it back inside the blanket. "You are already a fighter, my son. God has indeed replaced Onan and Er. He has given me back the heritage I believed He took from me. The God of my father has taken my actions and turned them to blessing. How great is the One God." He bowed his head over Tamar's hands. My eyes were damp. When he looked at the woman he smiled. She returned the smile with tears in her eyes. "Rest." He touched her hair gently and stood up.

I watched my son leave the tent and heard him shouting the news to the camp.

"Tamar has been delivered of healthy twin sons. Rejoice, for the God of my father Israel is gracious and restores what was lost!"

Dinah smiled at her brother's words. She sighed softly as she ran a gentle finger over Perez' forehead. "My sister, you are indeed blessed. I will never know the love of a husband or bear sons." I saw a tear glistening in her eyes as she slipped past me to join the celebration with Judah and his brothers.

# Chapter 16

Dinah's words reminded me of her lonely life. I spoke to Jacob a few days later. "My husband, your daughter Dinah remains unwed. Surely God would not want her to remain a widow forever."

"A widow?" he questioned, turning in surprise.

"It was from her marriage bed that she was rescued," I pointed out. "Shechem had paid the bride price you set."

Jacob stood looking first at me and then across the compound to where Dinah sat with Tamar and the babies. I could tell that he was thinking. "That is true," he acknowledged finally. "I had not thought that you would wish a husband for Dinah."

"I think Tamar's twins have reminded her of how much she has missed by not being a mother," I replied. "Haven't you seen how she is always helping with the children?"

"Who would you choose for her husband?" The question was a challenge.

"There is a young man from Hebron, the son of Jonah the merchant, who I believe has an interest in our daughter."

"We will see about this." I could not tell if her father was happy or angry as he strode across the camp to stand in front of Dinah. "Daughter, I am told that there is a young man in Hebron. Is it true that you have an interest in him?"

The woman's face turned rosy and she glared at me. Then proudly she lifted her chin. "Yes, my father, Abarim and I have spoken. He knows that I am ..." She stumbled on the words. "I was ... Shechem ..."

"Very well." Surprisingly, Jacob took pity on her stammering. "I will speak to Jonah and Abarim." Then he smiled at her. "Perhaps my Dinah will be a bride." He patted her shoulder and walked away leaving his daughter staring after him.

"How dare you? How did you know?" She turned on me torn between anger and hope. "Will Father really speak to Abarim?"

"He has said so." I shrugged, answering only the last question. "I am sure he will." In my heart I wondered what Jonah would say about his son marrying a woman older than most brides and a widow.

"Not that she is old," I reminded myself. "I was bearing sons when I was her age. Surely Dinah deserves a family."

It was late when Jacob returned. I could tell that many cups of the local barley beer had been consumed. That could only mean good news. My feet were light as I hurried to the man. "What did Jonah say?" I asked impatiently. My husband steadied himself on my arm and rested one hand on the donkey's back.

"Dinah will be a bride at the full moon."

It was the answer I prayed for. "We will begin preparations at once." I smiled in the darkness.

"Yes, it will be a great feast." He staggered slightly, and I guided him to a seat by the fire. "Rejoice for your sister, my sons," Jacob announced to the men lounging there. "Dinah will be wed to Abarim, son of Jonah the merchant, at the time of the full moon." Surprised questions burst from many lips to be quieted by the raised hand of their father. "My sons, all is decided. The young man knows that your sister is a widow not a virgin. He loves her in spite of that."

"Widow?" Levi asked in surprise, echoing his father's earlier question.

"Yes." Jacob's answer rang with authority even though it was my words he repeated. "It was from her marriage bed that she was taken."

Four men looked at each other but no one said anything as Jacob reminded them, "Shechem had paid the bride price."

Suddenly Reuben gave a hoot of laughter. "Father, you are shrewd. Who else would have looked at Dinah's time with Shechem in that way?"

Jacob glanced at me. I hid a grin behind my hand. "I will go tell Dinah," I said leaving the men to celebrate far into the night.

Bilhah and Zilpah joyfully joined in the baking and chopping required for the bridal feast. Dinah fluttered about in a state of unusual nervousness and excitement. Tamar kept her busy and helped her pack the leather chest. She folded and refolded her clothing and blankets so many times I feared they would be worn out.

At last the day of the full moon came. With loving hands, I dressed my daughter. Jacob had purchased a new embroidered and beaded gown. My hands shook as I arranged the veil on her braided hair.

"Is my daughter ready?" Jacob's voice called through the tent walls.

Zilpah lifted the tent flap. Dinah's father held a heavy necklace ornamented with copper coins. My eyes opened wide at the weight of the gift. She would never be in want with such a dowry.

"Dinah, my daughter." His eyes were tender as he fastened the jewelry at her neck. "May the God of my fathers, the One God who called me Israel, grant you the same wealth of children that he has fulfilled in me." He took her by the shoulders and then bent forward to kiss her on the forehead, "Never have I seen a lovelier bride."

Through the veil, I could see her radiant blush. She lowered her head. Touching the necklace, she whispered, "Thank you Father, you are so good to me." Impulsively Dinah threw her arms around her father's neck and kissed him.

"Your brothers, too, have gifts." The man seemed taken aback by her emotion.

Ten men trooped in with their presents. Suddenly the tent seemed very small. They hugged their sister and presented her with gifts of hammered copper and soft leather. Then Benjamin called her to the door where he stood. "We all made this!" He proudly waved his hand toward the bridal litter.

Tears choked her voice as Dinah thanked her brothers. The sound of music and chanting reminded us that the groom was approaching. Jacob lifted his daughter into the litter. With a final kiss he lowered the curtains. Reuben and Simeon took the front with Levi and Judah at the back. Together, they lifted the litter. Surrounded by her brothers and escorted by Jacob, Dinah set out to meet Abarim and the men from town. Then the entire crowd marched to the feasting tents set up between our tents and Hebron. Dinah was now carried by Abarim's groomsmen while he walked beside the litter. Jacob and his sons followed to where the massive feast was laid out. The day of feasting, song, and dance passed too swiftly for me. The setting sun saw Abarim leading his bride to the wedding tent. My heart caught in my throat as I saw her place her hand trustingly in his. Amid the cheers of the crowd and the clashing of instruments, the couple walked to their tent.

The night was old when I made my way from the feast toward my tent. Lost in my memories of forty years earlier, I didn't see Jacob. "My wife, will our daughter be happy?" His voice surprised me. He was standing beside the path staring at the white tent clearly visible in the moonlight.

"She loves him and he seems to love her," I replied, wondering why he asked.

"Are you happy?" The next question was even more surprising. I was unsure how to answer. My mind raced to form a reply. He took me gently by the shoulders as he had Dinah earlier. It made my heart race and I felt myself quiver at his touch. "Leah?" Like a boy he seemed unsure of himself as he bent his head to try to see my face. "Are you happy?"

"Why would I not be?" I tried to quiet my whirling thoughts and hedged my answer. The night shadows hid my face so he couldn't see my telltale eyes. I was glad because they would have said what I was afraid to put into words: Jacob, my husband, I do love you. I am only happy when you love me. Your touch makes my heart race."

The man sighed and dropped his hands. He turned away and I knew I failed to give him the answer he sought. I whispered his name but he didn't hear and continued to walk toward his tent with his head bowed. In my tent, I cried myself to sleep like a maiden. Too many years of seeing myself rejected silenced my tongue. In the morning light, I wanted to reopen the conversation but didn't know how. So, I watched him as he moved about the camp, playing with the children and then joining our sons to check the herds.

Dinah's bridal week came to an end. Occasionally, I went to Hebron. Dinah was glowing with happiness and before fall she was pregnant. A baby boy was born in late spring. They named him Jacob. His grandfather was ecstatic.

Benjamin, too, found a wife. I was surprised when Jacob gave permission for Rachel's surviving son to marry. For his entire life he had been sheltered, and his father seldom let him out of his sight or out of camp.

"You look so much like your mother," he often told the young man. "Both you and Joseph have hair and eyes like Rachel's. I will not let anything happen to you. You must stay close by as a comfort to my old age."

The winter morning was clear and cold when Benjamin approached his father by the fire.

"My father, I have found a girl I desire to marry," he stated boldly.

Jacob looked up from his breakfast. Levi and Judah stared at their brother. I held my breath to see what the response would be.

"Really?" The man's answer seemed to give his son encouragement.

"Yes," he nodded, falling to his knees beside his father. "She is the daughter of Hiram of Bethel. Her name is Debora."

"How did you meet this girl?" Jacob asked frowning at the young man.

He did not quail before the look. Lifting his chin Benjamin responded, "We met last year when you went to Bethel to worship. Her father trades at Hebron sometimes and is there now."

"Have you spoken to her father?" The frown deepened.

"No bride price has been discussed." For the first time, the son didn't look at his father.

Jacob stood up. "You have gone behind my back to seek out a wife! You have spoken to her father! The man will expect a visit from me!" I was not surprised by the anger. It was fueled by fear of losing the last vestige of Rachel.

Benjamin sprang up to face his father, "Yes, I have found a girl I will marry!" His passion was equal to his father's. "You did not deny my brothers wives from our neighbors. I am of more than an age to marry. Even Dinah has been given the joy of a household and child."

My husband was taken aback by his son's vehemence. Helplessly, he looked at me. "Hiram is well thought of. I am sure the girl is sweet." My words sought to bridge the gap between the two men. "She will come and live with us just as all the wives of your other sons have. You will have the joy of many more grandchildren. Perhaps even daughters who will look like my sister." The last words almost choked me, but they made Jacob nod.

He turned back to his son. Benjamin stood belligerently watching his father. "I will speak to Hiram of Bethel," he assured the young man. "We will arrange the details. My youngest son will be a groom."

"Thank you, Father." Gratefully, the young man hugged his father. Jacob's face was not happy, but in his excitement, the boy didn't notice.

So it was that before the winter ended, Benjamin married Debora. She proved to be a lovely and gentle girl. Her first son was born in the early fall. Twins followed the next year. My heart was full whenever I held one of my grandchildren. There were so many now that the camp seemed to have more children than adults sometimes. My heart overflowed as I watched the families prosper. My husband often came to my tent at night. I was content in my role of matriarch and told myself that it didn't matter that I never heard the words I longed to hear.

# Chapter 17

It seemed that the One God was indeed blessing us. Year after year, there were wonderful harvests. Grazing was plentiful from Damascus to the Negev. The flocks and herds grew in number every year. My sons spread out and grazed their animals in many different valleys. They were able to sell the animals and the hides for great profit. My sons grew rich and Jacob was honored by all in Canaan. At the spring moon, everyone came together for the journey to Bethel, where Jacob renewed his vows to the God who called him Israel. Monthly sacrifices were made at the altar in Hebron.

Benjamin was twenty-six when the drought began. At first, everyone thought it was just a dry winter. Even on the heights to the north there was no snow. The spring rains didn't come. The lambs were stillborn and the camels miscarried. At Bethel, Jacob prayed for rain. We stayed at the shrine while Jacob joined with the elders of the city in petition. The summer brought no moisture and the weaker animals began to die. Our stores of grain began to be rationed within the camp. Reuben and Judah came to their father.

"We must look further north," they said. "Perhaps there is still grazing and water there."

Jacob nodded, "I have heard that there is grass beyond Shechem. May the God of Abraham the Wanderer and Isaac the Shepherd be with you to find good land. Scout out a place for the animals, and then together we will herd them there."

My two oldest sons set out. Benjamin begged to accompany them. "Father, let me go. My flocks are failing too," he pleaded.

"No, my son." The gray beard flowed from side to side with the intensity of the man's refusal. "I could not bear to lose you to the north as I lost your brother. Reuben and Judah will find grazing for us all."

Before a moon cycle, they returned. Eagerly, everyone gathered to hear the report. "My father," Reuben stated, "there is no more water or grazing to the north than here." A whisper that was almost a moan came from the listening tribe. He added, "The word among the caravans is that only in Egypt is there food."

Judah interrupted, "The food can be bought. They have grain for man and beast."

"Is there no drought in Egypt?" Jacob wanted to know.

"We heard from the traders that even though the drought is severe in Egypt a wise Governor made preparation for this famine. Something about a dream of Pharaoh that prepared them." Reuben's reply caused Jacob to shake his head.

"Why did not the God of my fathers send us a messenger to prepare us?"

No one could answer. Levi spoke up when the silence stretched out, "My father, we can go to Egypt and buy food for our families."

Judah nodded eagerly, "Yes, everyone we talked to agreed that the Governor will sell to any who comes." He paused and added, "It will cost a great deal to buy food for us all."

"Am I a poor man that such things should trouble me?" Jacob growled. "I am saddened that my sons should have to beg for food like rabble."

"Perhaps," I bent close to my husband, "perhaps the God who has made you rich has provided the grain in Egypt to preserve your life."

He tapped his fingers together and stroked his chin. For a long time he gazed across the plain to the mountains. Silently, the men, their families, and their servants awaited his decision. "How much is the cost of the grain?" He finally turned to look at Reuben and Judah.

"A month's supply of grain for one family costs one shekel weight for an Egyptian. It is five times that for a foreigner," Judah replied.

All eyes were fixed on the sheik. He sighed and sat down heavily. "You will all go. All except Benjamin," he declared waving his hand to include ten sons. "Buy as much grain as you can with the silver I will send with you."

Benjamin opened his mouth to argue but resisted when he saw his father bow his head into his hands. The defeated posture made me kneel beside my husband and stroke his arm.

"Why did God choose to warn the Egyptians and not me?" His voice was ragged with anguish.

"My husband, who can understand the mind of your God. Surely there is a purpose that we don't understand." My words seemed empty even as I attempted to comfort the man.

"Leah, you are always faithful." He turned his head to look at me. "How can you trust even now? God is taking away everything he gave me? My flocks and herds are dying in front of my eyes and my grandchildren cry for food. I am sending my sons to Egypt. Who knows if I will see them again?"

"God has never abandoned you," I pointed out. Even in the moment, I rejoiced that their father at last acknowledged that he cared for all his sons. "When my father cheated you, your God blessed you. You were protected from Esau's vengeance and have gained honor that is more than wealth among all in Canaan. God himself called you Israel because you fought with God and won."

"Yet, if my sons are gone, I will have nothing left." He bowed his head again. .

"God will bring them back safely," I promised, and in that moment I knew that it was not just a platitude to soothe his heart, but the truth I believed. Dawn was not even breaking when the ten men set out. They rode the donkeys that would carry home the grain. "May the God of Israel, your father, bring you back safely to him." My prayer followed them down the dusty road.

Waiting for their return was hard. Each day I scanned the road knowing that it would be at least three moons cycles before they could return. Benjamin seemed content to remain in camp. He accompanied his father daily to the altar where Jacob spent hours in prayer seeking to hear God's voice. My heart wept for his desolation, and I prayed for words to comfort him with. God remained as silent as the dark cloudless skies that the man stared at night after night. I knew he was reminded of the promises to Abraham and Isaac. The daily sight of the hungry animals and children tortured him.

At long last, we saw a cloud of dust approaching which eventually revealed nine men and donkeys. My hand went to my throat as I hurried to meet my sons.

Jacob asked the question first. "Where is your brother? Where is Simeon?" A babble of voices tried to answer at once. The man held up his hand and sank into his seat in front of the tent. He put his head into his hands and wailed. "I have lost another son. God is punishing me."

Hurrying to his side, I knelt and put my hand on his knee. "No, my husband, Simeon cannot be dead." I turned to Reuben for confirmation.

He stepped forward, "Father, it is true, Simeon is not dead."

The man raised his head, "Then where is my son?"

Asher blurted out, "In the Governor's jail."

Jacob flinched as though struck and his voice was gruff as he spoke one word, "How?"

Judah stepped up as spokesman when all the brothers looked at each other. "Father, we traveled to Egypt as you directed. The journey was hard, for the water holes were scarce. Border guards questioned us rigorously. They directed us to Memphis where the royal business is conducted."

He paused and Zebulon interjected, "The land is amazing, even in famine. There are such buildings and paintings and carvings as you have never seen!" He shook his shaggy head in amazement at the wonders he had noticed.

"Yes, and the women," Asher began, only to stop at a nudge from his brother who nodded toward the gathered wives. Zilpah's youngest son gulped and grinned sheepishly.

Judah spoke hurriedly, "We trudged up to Memphis late one night. Outside the gate, we were shown where to camp. In the morning, we requested an audience with the Governor." He shook his head as he continued. "The magnificence of the palace you cannot imagine." Awed tones told the story. "We were led down a long hall. It was wider than your tent, Father," his hand gestured to the hide shelter. The entire camp was spellbound by his narration. "The floor shown like a smooth lake on a clear day. We could see our dusty tracks as we walked along. Silent servants in white linen loincloths moved past us carrying fans and trays of food."

"They acted like we were contaminated," Gad inserted a little angrily. "Just because we are hairy and they have no hair."

Judah looked briefly at his brother then resumed. "The steward led us to a huge door. It was made of some black wood and taller than the cedars on the hills. There were gold shields on the panels. One side opened and we walked in five abreast. The hall was so large that our whole encampment would fit inside it." A collective gasp greeted his words. Jacob raised his eyebrows and looked around at his many tents. I tried to imagine a room that would hold them all. It was impossible. "As we stood staring at the paintings and gold, the Governor strode past us with his guard and fan bearer. He stood on the dais and looked down at us. Of course, we fell face down before such majesty."

Jacob growled, "That my sons should have to endure such shame!"

Judah tilted his head as he explained, "The man was very stern looking and his gold regalia caught the light so that he was like a god. Then the ruler sent for an interpreter and questioned us."

"Could he not see that you were honest men in need of food?" Again the father took umbrage at the insult.

"My father," Levi replied, "if you could have seen the land and the people," after a pause he added, "surely, to the Governor we looked poor and strange."

"Let Judah continue," I urged, still wondering why my Simeon was in an Egyptian jail. I could see his wife wringing her hands as the other women comforted her.

At his father's nod, Judah took up the tale. "The man asked us where we were from and if we had other kin. He seemed most interested in you, Father. Twice he asked us if our father was indeed still alive." Judah stopped speaking. With a deep breath and a glance at the women and children he continued, "Then he accused us of being spies and put us all in jail for three days."

My husband half rose from his seat, "The Egyptian put my sons in jail?"

"It wasn't so bad," Issachar said. "Just a big room with a dirt floor and a locked door. The guards brought us bread and water twice a day."

"How did you get out?" Jacob settled back into his seat.

"After three days," Judah answered, "the Governor sent for us. He said, "I fear God and would not have your children die because of your lies. I will give you the food you want." We were so grateful that we fell down at his feet and thanked him. Then the man told us, "However, as surety for your honesty, one brother will remain in jail here in Egypt. When you bring to me the youngest brother you claim to have, then I will believe that you are not spies. You will never see this brother again if the boy is not with you when you return." Guards immediately surrounded Simeon. They bound him and led him away. Reuben tried to plead with the Governor, but he refused to listen. Instead, he left the room. A slave boy came and led us to the granary where our bags were filled. Then the lad escorted us to the border by a shorter route than we came."

Simeon's wife was weeping openly and I felt tears stinging my eyes.

"Then my son is lost to me." Jacob bowed his head into his chest.

Reuben spoke up, "Not so my father. When Benjamin returns with us, Simeon will be freed."

"No." Adamantly the head shook from side to side.

"Also, Father," Judah added, holding out the leather pouch that carried the silver to Egypt as a purchase price, "our silver was somehow put back in our sacks. We gave it to the Governor, but at our first camp outside of Egypt, we found it in the grain when we made our meal."

"I see now." The old man reared to his feet to pace in rage. "It is a trick. Should you return to Egypt, the Governor will use that as an excuse to enslave or kill you all. I will not risk losing all my sons." He drew Benjamin close to his side and stalked into his tent. The flap fell into place behind him with finality. I was left looking at the nine men. Confusion and anger were clear on their faces. My eyes reflected the rage I felt again at Rachel and Joseph and Benjamin. Fifteen years of fellowship and intimacy between Jacob and his sons was lost in the instant that Rachel's son was threatened. The respect and fondness I thought I had found with my husband were swept away in the dry, desert wind. While he had never said that he loved me, he had chosen my bed many nights, and I thought there was affection in his heart. The closing of his tent flap echoed in my heart. Once again I was shut out.

Levi snarled, "Always the favorite is protected. First it was Joseph and now Benjamin can't be risked. When the grain is gone, we will all die."

I moved away to my tent as the men turned to unload the donkeys. Angrily I stormed at God, "God of my husband, why do you allow this? My son, Simeon, will die in an Egyptian jail so that Jacob can protect all that is left of his beloved Rachel. His other sons are worth more than either of my sister's spoiled sons. Even in death, Rachel and Joseph stand between my husband and me. He will let us starve rather than let Benjamin out of his sight." I wept in rage and fear. "God, if you care, send rains and harvests so that we do not starve. Bring Simeon back to his family and me."

# Chapter 18

I did not sleep well. The next morning I questioned Reuben and Judah about their brother. "Tell me again what happened in Egypt." The men stood in front of me.

"First, the Governor accused us all of being spies," Judah answered.

"We tried to explain that we were ten brothers," Reuben inserted. "He just stared at us. There was the coldest expression on his face," he shuddered at the memory, "like we were beneath contempt and worse than the mud his servants scraped from his sandals." Levi added as he joined the group in front of my tent.

"What else did he say?" I insisted on hearing it all again.

"The Governor didn't believe we were brothers," Reuben resumed the narrative. "I guess we don't look enough alike."

"You all have the look of Jacob," I said, fondly looking from face to face. "All Jacob's sons have his eyes and square face." Except Rachel's sons, I added to myself, who inherited her wavy hair and rounder face. I hoped no one noticed the resentment in my eyes as I thought of my sister's favored sons.

"The Governor questioned us about our families and then said, 'Put these men in jail. I will look into their case when I have more time.'" Judah spoke the words coldly, just as the Egyptian had spoken them. "You can't imagine the terror we felt to hear those words. Guards with spears and swords surrounded us. Our own daggers were taken from us. They marched us to the jail. It was more like a pit than a room. Through the grate in the ceiling, food and water were let down. We saw the sun cross the floor three times. On the fourth morning, we were ordered out and brought before the Governor again."

"This time," Reuben interrupted, "the man seemed more amiable. He said, 'I fear God and would not want women and children to suffer because of your lies.' "

He paused for breath and Levi spoke, "Then the guards grabbed Simeon. They bound his hands and took him away. It was all very sudden. We were told 'If you return with the youngest brother you claim to have, I will believe that you are indeed kin. Otherwise that man who you say is your brother will die.' "

Reuben suddenly fell at my feet. "Mother it is all my fault."

Before I could answer, Judah and Levi grabbed his shoulders and arms to drag him away. "Fool," Judah hissed.

"Be still," Levi ordered.

"No!" My first-born shook off their hands. "I didn't heed my brother's pleas and now we are all punished."

"What could you have done to save Simeon?" I looked at my son in surprise.

"Not Simeon." He shook his head. Tormented eyes looked up into mine. He took my hands. "Mother, I refused to listen to Joseph's cry for mercy. This is God's punishment. My own brother is taken from me and my children will die of starvation."

"What do you mean?" The words were barely a whisper as a terrible fear flooded over me. My eyes must have betrayed my horror.

"We didn't kill him," Judah hastened to reassure me.

Without speaking, I looked at each man in turn.

"He found us in Dothan." Reuben's voice was expressionless as he recited the crime. "We were still angry about the dreams he bragged of and the coat he flaunted. Nothing we did was good enough, but Joseph got special treatment just because he was Joseph." The big man shook his head sadly. "We saw him coming and decided to teach him a lesson. So we ..." he ran his hands restlessly through his hair as he paused.

Levi interrupted, "We tore off the coat, beat him and threw him into the dry well. It was just to teach him that he wasn't the most important one. He was too arrogant."

"He called out to me." Reuben gripped his ears and rocked back and forth as though trying to block out the memory of Joseph's words. "The words have haunted me all these years. 'Reuben, my brother, would you do this to your own brother?'" Levi and Judah placed a hand on their brother's shoulder. "I ran away from his cries. I left the camp and the sheep. I fled to the hills. Still I heard his voice calling my name." Tears ran down his cheeks into his beard. He gripped my hands tightly as he finished the story. "When I returned to camp, Joseph was gone from the well. At first, I thought my brothers had sent him on his way. Then I learned the truth."

Judah joined his brother at my knees. "Mother, we sold Joseph to slave traders on their way to Egypt. It seemed the perfect opportunity to get rid of him forever. Never again would he lord it over us or tattle to Father. We never thought of our father or what would happen to our brother."

My throat constricted and I could hardly breath.

Levi knelt beside his brothers and confessed, "We divided the money. Then Simeon ripped the fancy coat and used goat's blood to make it look like our brother was killed by wild animals."

Reuben buried his face in his hands. "Now this is God's punishment on me. I did not rescue Joseph when I had the chance. My own family will die and I with them."

My mind was whirling with the shock of the news. Absentmindedly, I stroked each bowed head. More than twenty years had slipped by. There could be no purpose served by telling Jacob that his son was not killed by beasts, but was sold into slavery. After twenty years he would not be alive. Slavery would not have suited the proud young man. Frantically, my mind raced in all directions like a frightened rabbit. My sons had committed a crime against their half-brother. Perhaps this famine was a punishment. I knew I couldn't tell Jacob, but I didn't know what to do.

"There must be a way to get Simeon back and even buy more food." Levi's words returned my thoughts to the current crisis.

"Unless Benjamin returns with us to Egypt, we have no hope," Judah reminded him.

In a daze, I walked away from the camp. Somehow I found myself near the altar Jacob built. The well-used pile of rocks reminded me of his faith and of his God. "God of my husband, God of Jacob, you promised him blessings. Why do you steal his sons from him? Joseph and Simeon are both lost to Egypt." I found myself crying as remorse swept over me. "What have I done? God of Israel, my own hatred has come back against me. Because I did not mourn for Joseph, my own son is taken." Crouching next to the altar, I wept for Simeon and for Joseph. "Forgive me," I pleaded, "in my malice against my sister and her son I have brought disaster on my husband and my sons. I am guiltier than Reuben and Judah. It was my rage they learned and that turned them against their brother." I cried until I was weak. The stars came out in the cold, empty sky. I felt no comfort or peace. "God," I begged, "do not forsake your servant Jacob because of my sins. Take me and restore his sons to him."

Reuben found me huddled next to the altar and half carried me to my tent. Zilpah was waiting. Her face relaxed in relief when she saw me. I let her put me to bed.

The morning didn't ease the emptiness I felt. Like a shell I went about the daily tasks including measuring out the grain so it would last as long as possible. Jacob's praise of my diligence brought no warmth to my heart. I wished I dared throw myself into his arms and sob out a confession. The words wouldn't even come to urge my husband to send his sons to Egypt. Rescuing Simeon and buying more grain seemed impossible. My newly realized guilt hung over me like a cloud. I felt unworthy of approaching God or man with my petitions. The grain supply decreased slowly and each day we all prayed for rain. The brilliant sun continued to shine, shriveling the few brave sprouts in the spring. Few lambs were born, and the flocks were so small and weak that it only took a couple of the boys to watch them. Grazing narrowed to thin strips beside the little remaining water. It was the sight of my grandchildren's thin arms that helped me find my voice. "My husband." The words sounded distant to my ears, but he looked up from the leather he was sewing.

"Leah, my wife, you have been silent lately." His voice held a gentle concern that was unexpected. It brought tears to my eyes.

"I have been busy," I murmured as an excuse.

"You are troubled about Simeon," he stated.

It was my opportunity. "Yes, I am concerned about our son and the food supply. The grain is almost gone. There will be no crop again this year." I stated the obvious, looking beyond my husband to the barren, brown hillsides.

"I will send my sons to Egypt again," he announced decisively.

"Benjamin, too?" I asked hopefully.

"No, the boy will stay here."

When I opened my mouth to protest the man stood up. "I will speak to Reuben and Judah tonight. We have delayed too long already." True to his word, he called his sons together at his tent. In the moonlight, the thinness of their faces stood out in stark relief. Like me, they had been limiting their ration so the women and children could have more. I wondered briefly if guilt kept them from eating, like it did me. "The grain you brought from Egypt is almost gone," Jacob's deep voice drew the men's attention. "There will be no harvest this fall."

I saw nods of agreement from the nine men. "Then we are to go to Egypt again?" Reuben spoke for all.

"Yes, get grain for another year. Surely God will send rain in the spring and we will have food here in Canaan." The old man stood up only to be halted by Reuben's words.

"Father, will you send Benjamin? It is of no use for us to go if he is not with us."

Angrily shaking his head, the reply was vehement. "He alone is left of Rachel. Joseph is no more. He was killed by wild beasts in his youth. Simeon you have lost to Egypt. No, I will not let you take Benjamin. Without my sons, I am bereft."

"I have two sons," Reuben pleaded, kneeling before his father. "Take them as a guarantee of my return with Benjamin. Put him in my charge, and I will bring him safely back to you."

Still the gray head shook in denial, "No, Benjamin will not leave my sight!"

"Then there is no reason for us to go to Egypt. Better we stay here with our families so we can die together." Reuben angrily marched from his father's presence followed by his brothers. Benjamin remained standing in front of Jacob.

"Please, my father, let me go with my brothers. We need the food. They have said that the Governor will not even talk to them unless I am with them."

"No, my son." The answer was gruff and Jacob tried to soften the reply. "I cannot risk losing you." With a sob in his voice he finished, "I see Rachel when I look at you. To my sorrow, I gave in to your brother's pleas and he is dead. If I lost you, I would die."

"Yes, Father." Head bowed, the young man sadly walked away.

I confronted my husband as he stared after Benjamin. "If you do not send to Egypt for food, we will all die. Your sons and their wives and children will starve. Even precious Benjamin will waste away before your eyes."

He turned to look at me. "You do not understand," he began.

"No," heatedly I interrupted, "I do understand. I know how you cling to Rachel's memory even as we all die in this famine. The flocks are dying from lack of grazing. There is no food anywhere except in Egypt. In holding onto the losses of the past, you will lose any hope for the future." Jacob turned his back, but I continued, "Do you think you are better than Abraham the Wanderer? Did not your God ask Abraham to sacrifice his precious and only son?" I was almost screaming. Then I lowered my voice, "Your God gave him his son again."

"The son of the promise is dead already," the man growled.

"Who can know the ways of God?" Remembering my sons' confession I added, "Perhaps Joseph is not dead."

Jacob sank back into the seat. He rocked back and forth with his head in his hands. "Benjamin is Rachel's son, my youngest. God, why do you ask of me my most precious possession?"

I almost stamped my foot in frustration, "God has promised you an inheritance. Where is that heritage if we all die of starvation?"

"I must think." The voice was tired and I watched him walk slowly out of camp to the altar. What happened there I never knew. In the morning, he again called his sons together. "You must go to Egypt or we will all perish."

This time it was Judah who spoke. "The Governor of the land warned us that without our youngest brother we would never see his face again. Unless Benjamin is with us, we will be unable to buy grain."

Again Jacob bowed his head in his hands. "If I lose my son, I will die. Why did you have to tell the Governor that you had another brother?" The words came out as a desperate cry.

"He asked us if we had a father or any other brothers." Judah shrugged. "How were we to know he would order us to bring our youngest brother to his court? He could just as easily have required you to come."

"That I would readily have done." Bleakly the old man peered at Judah.

"Father, I know the grief of the loss of a child. I have lost two sons," the man reminded his father. "Entrust Benjamin to me, I will bring him safe to you again." I was proud of my son as he placed his hands together across his chest in an oath. "If I do not bring my brother back to you, I will bear the blame forever. May the God of Abraham and Isaac and Jacob be witness that on me will come the punishment of the betrayal of this vow."

Slowly, as though forced, Jacob nodded. "Then do this also. Take some balm and nuts from Canaan as a gift to the Governor. Take the first payment and extra silver for more grain. Explain to the Egyptian that the money was returned by accident before he accuses you all of being thieves."

"Yes, Father," Judah bowed to his father. "If we had not waited so long, we would have already returned."

"Take Benjamin and go." The old man turned and entered his tent. "If my son is lost, surely I will die."

I hurried to gather a magnificent gift for the Governor. Balm and nuts and woven goods were placed in a handsome leather trunk. "Here is the gift for the Governor," I told Levi. With a hug for each son, I bid them goodbye and watched them walk away from camp leading the little donkeys. Weakened by the scant grazing, the little beasts couldn't be ridden. "God of Jacob," I whispered, "be with them and bring them all safely back to your servant Israel. He has given you his all. Do not take it from him."

I could not know that God was indeed going to restore everything to my husband. Slowly, I turned back to the camp to face the thin faces and hungry eyes of the tribe.

# Chapter 19

My heart ached for Jacob. Day by day he seemed to sink more into himself. I tried to interest him in the grandchildren but he simply turned his head away to gaze down the road to the south. Impatient for word, we moved the camp south to Hebron and then south again toward Beersheba. It was slow going because neither the animals nor shepherds had strength to go far each day.

"My husband, will not the God of your fathers bring them back safely?" I asked.

"God has asked for my heart's desire," was the answer.

"Have you forgotten God's promise at Bethel?" It was the covenant I clung to.

"What does that matter now? Rachel died bearing Benjamin. I buried her at Ephrath. Her sons were all I had left of my bride. Now both are gone. How could God demand all that I have ever loved?"

My sympathy was almost lost in the surge of the old jealous anger I thought was buried and gone. In a choked voice I reminded the man, "You received twelve sons from God."

He shook his head. "Rachel's were special."

"Because they were Rachel's?" The bitter words were out of my mouth before I could stop them.

Surprised, he raised his head. "The children of the barren are doubly blessed. Leah, you know that is true."

The words didn't ease the pain in my soul. Once again, my sons and I were second best. My offering of self was not enough. Even the God that I cried out to had never responded. "No." My reply was low and angry. "I have never understood why no matter what I do or my sons do, it is not enough." The confused look only increased my distress. Now that I had started, the words poured out. "Neither Laban nor you have ever seen me as anything more than the obedient workhorse who keeps everything in order. My sister could be beautiful and play with the sheep because responsible Leah would keep the household running smoothly. Rachel was barren, but it was not really a hardship because I bore you sons. Then, suddenly she had a son. He was placed above his brothers and given special honor. Is it any wonder they hated him?" Jacob opened his mouth but I couldn't stop. The agony of decades poured out as I confessed. "I learned about your God hoping you would love me. I bore you sons, kept your household, raised Rachel's sons, and never once have you looked at me with the love reserved for my sister. I hoped that after she died, you might come to love me. May your God forgive me, I let my jealousy infect my sons." My voice cracked and tears threatened as I rushed on. I couldn't even look at the man who was my mate. "You are not as concerned with Simeon in the Egyptian jail as with keeping Benjamin safe. Simeon, your second born son, could be dead for all you care. You are worried about Benjamin because he is Rachel's child. 'All I have left.' " I mimicked his words. "I have prayed to your God for the safe return of all your sons. Perhaps he will honor the prayer of a despised woman, even one such as me."

Embarrassed by my emotional outburst, I hurried away to my tent. I never dreamed that Jacob would follow me. On my bed, I sobbed out the last vestige of the despair and anger left in me. A hand on my shoulder caused me to roll away and curl into a ball. "Go away Zilpah. I want to be alone." The order was rough with tears.

"It is not Zilpah." My husband's voice startled me. Fear of what he would say made me curl more tightly against myself.

Surprisingly, he pulled me into his arms. Without a word he patted my back as though I was a child. Gradually, my sobs ceased. "I have wronged you, my wife," the words were gentle. "You are right in saying that I took you and your sons for granted. Your strong boys never needed my guidance with you as their mother."

"They wanted your love," I whispered.

"So did you, Leah of the lovely eyes." He tilted my head up with one finger. "I have known of your faith, my Leah. Your eyes glow with it when you talk of the One God or listen to me prate on about my visions." He shook his head. The brown eyes were ashamed. "Why did I never see that you loved me?"

The gentleness of my husband's voice and his hand smoothing my hair opened the floodgates of my tears again. I sobbed away the years of loneliness. The days when I believed Jacob loved only Rachel were washed away as I let the man comfort me. Eventually, my tears stopped and I dozed in his arms.

The morning light awakened me. Sitting up, I wondered if the loving care of Jacob had been a dream. He leaned against a pile of cushions. At my movement, I saw him look up. The smile and hand he held out to me assured me that his tenderness was real. Hesitantly, I leaned toward my husband. "Leah, my strong and faithful wife," he greeted me. "Did you sleep well?"

I nodded, too bemused by the expression in his eyes to speak. The next few days were the marriage week I never had. Together we walked the hills and visited the altar. Hand in hand we prayed for our sons' safe return. Each night he came to my tent, not out of duty, but with love.

Zilpah rejoiced with me. "My mistress is lovely. The master's love has made you young again."

All I could do was smile and nod, for indeed I felt like a bride. In Jacob's arms I was able to forget that my sons were in Egypt and that our grain supply was dwindling each day. Too soon the responsibilities of the camp encroached on our time. My presence was needed to help deliver Zebulon's newest son. Jacob was called away to meet with the elders in Beersheba about the scant water. He grew distracted once again. His eyes searched the southern road daily.

Jacob sought assurance from me one night, "Surely our sons are returning now from Egypt."

"If the journey went smoothly and the donkeys are strong enough, they should be here by the new moon rising," I replied, quickly calculating in my head and winging a prayer to God for their safety.

The new moon passed and the sliver of silver in the night grew to half before we saw dust on the horizon. Issachar's oldest child was the first to spread the news. He ran into the camp. "Look, a cloud of dust to the south! Is it a storm?"

Jacob hurried to look. I followed. Dust storms had plagued the dry land. The whirling, stinging clouds knocked down tents and coated everything with dirt.

Shading his eyes with his hand, the man squinted at the billowing dust. He turned with a frown. "It is not a storm. Perhaps it is a large caravan."

Relieved, the women went back to their chores. I watched my husband turn back to stare at the approaching plume.

"It could be an army to raise so much dust," he murmured.

"You don't think it is our sons?" I asked.

"A dozen donkeys do not make such a cloud, even with the roads so dry," he replied. His brow furrowed as he studied the rapidly approaching menace.

Suddenly, however, a lone figure was seen riding toward the camp. The man and donkey grew closer until I exclaimed, "It is Benjamin!"

The young man was excited when he reached us. Jumping from the donkey he grasped his father's shoulders. "We bring good news," he announced.

"Do you bring an army?" Jacob still stared beyond his son, even while enveloping him in a bear hug.

"No, we have wagons full of supplies. It is all part of the wonderful news."

"It is enough that you are here, my son!" The old man held Benjamin tightly. "Have all my sons returned?"

With a nod, the young man opened his mouth to speak, but he was forestalled by the arrival of his wife and the other women. Anything he wanted to say was lost in the welcoming chatter and eager questions by the rest of the camp. Shortly, ten more men rode into camp. As Benjamin promised, there were wagons with food supplies. The dark skinned Egyptian drivers looked startled at the roar of welcome from many mouths.

I stared in astonishment as the wagons were unloaded. We had such a feast. There were vegetables and new wine. Baskets of dried fish and sacks of grain were piled beside the wagons. We had not seen such bounty in years. It was late when everyone was fed. Sated with the food from Egypt, we gathered at Jacob's tent to hear from the travelers.

Reuben and Judah solicitously seated Jacob near the fire, for the evening was cool. Simeon led me to a seat next to my husband. Wives and children gathered to hear the story. The old man looked at the eleven men who squatted near him. They waited for him to ask for their tale. Benjamin's eyes sparkled with some magnificent secret and Levi placed a calming hand on his brother's shoulder.

"My sons," at last the chief of the tribe spoke, "I sent you to the Land of Kings to buy grain for a few months." He waved his hand toward the wagons tilted on their yokes. "You return with the bounty of the land and with slaves. Tell me how this has come about."

We all held our breath. Judah stood up. "My father," he began, "we have great news." He came close to Jacob and took his hand. With a glance at Benjamin, who watched impatiently, he continued. "Your son Joseph is alive."

The collective gasp of surprise echoed my own. Wildly, I stared from my son to my husband. Jacob sat stunned. His mouth opened slightly. In a low plea he said, "Do not lie to me."

"It is true!" Unable to restrain himself any longer, Benjamin leapt to his feet. He rushed to kneel beside Judah. Grabbing his father's hand he held it to his cheek. "I have seen my brother. He is alive."

"How?" The single word came out as a strangled sob.

"Joseph was not killed," my son stated. He paused to look at his brothers.

Reuben stood up. "Wild animals did not attack Joseph," he repeated. Jacob leaned forward to hear. "He was taken to Egypt where he was sold as a slave." Shamefaced, the two brothers looked at each other.

"A slave! My son is a slave in Egypt? I must ransom him!" In agitation, he struggled to rise. His distress kept him from asking how the favorite son of a great sheik came to be in a slave caravan.

I bowed my own head in despair. Jacob would hate all his sons and me now that the truth was told. Tears rose in my eyes and a lump formed in my throat as I clung to the memory of these past brief weeks of true love from my husband.

"Wait." Benjamin held on to his father. "Listen to all that God has done."

Judah took up the story. "Joseph has risen to be the Lord Governor of the land of Egypt. He has a new name. In Egypt, he is called Zaphenath-Paneah." He stumbled slightly over the odd name. "Your son is second only to Pharaoh."

Jacob sank back against the pillows. His words voiced my thoughts, "His dreams, my son dreamed this would happen." I heard joy begin to rise in his voice. "Don't you remember? Joseph dreamed that you and even his mother and I would bow to him. Indeed all the world bows to my son. The promises of God are true. God is indeed gracious!"

My heart turned to lead as I listened to my husband's praises. The child of the promise was restored. The beloved son was great and mighty as he always foretold. What need would he have for me now?

"There is more." Reuben took a step toward his father. "Joseph has seen that there will be five more years of this famine. That is why he sent all these wagons. We are to come to Egypt and live in the place he will give us."

"I will see my son again!" Jacob seemed to lose years. His smile was almost boyish as he stood to embrace each son in turn.

"We will indeed go to Egypt." The announcement was not a surprise. The strong voice rang out in the encampment. "My son lives and has prepared a place for us in this famine time!"

He turned to me. Lifting me to my feet, he drew me into his arms. "I will see my son before I die. As you said, God has returned all my sons to me."

Tears clouded my eyes and choked me. Unable to speak, I could only nod. My words had proved prophetic, but the reality left me bereft of hope for myself. Before long, Jacob would realize that it was my jealousy and rage that fed my sons' hatred of their brother. He would turn against me.

That night, I found myself crying in despair and remorse. "God of my husband, you return the dead to life. My hatred and jealousy of Rachel and her son caused his brothers to sell him. You are God. You are greater than I can comprehend. I see that you continue to bless your servant Jacob and that he has no need of me. Let me die now, before I see his fondness turn to loathing." I fell asleep eventually, tossing with troubled images dancing in my mind. In every dream Jacob spurned me and left me to die in the desert.

# Chapter 20

The dreams left me weak and feverish. I claimed I was ill from the surfeit of food after the famine, but my heart was broken. Even awake I saw the images from my dreams. They left me sweating and gasping in fear. In my mind, I saw Jacob turn from me to his son and saw Egyptian swords raised to destroy me. I knew Jacob would reject me for my part in Joseph's betrayal, and then I would die. Refusing to give in to the sick despair, I worked alongside Zilpah and Bilhah to prepare for the journey. There was a feeling of hope throughout the entire camp despite the meager, weakened flocks and herds. We remained near Beersheba preparing for the trek to Egypt. The water skins would be filled before we headed into the southern desert, the Negev.

Jacob came to see me one night. At first, I was afraid he had come to condemn me. "The God who met me at Bethel has spoken to me again," he began without preamble squatting by my side.

"Yes, my husband," I smiled encouragement, savoring each moment with the man before he thrust me from his sight.

"He has promised to go into Egypt with us and to bring us out again a great nation." His excitement was contagious. I even felt stronger. "The One God is not contained by boundaries. He has promised that we will come again to this land that He long ago promised to Abraham the Wanderer." Taking my hand, he smiled at me, "You, too, will come to Egypt and see Joseph and hold his children in your arms."

"My husband …" I wanted to beg his forgiveness and implore him not to reject me.

He interrupted, "Leah, I need you at my side. I am an old man. God has returned all my sons to me. You must be with me to share the joy." He pressed a kiss to my forehead before rising. "Rest and be well. Tomorrow we will journey back north to Hebron to offer sacrifices before heading to Egypt. We will tell Dinah that Joseph is alive and she will come with us. Even my daughter and her family will be saved from this famine."

With the first light, Benjamin lifted me into a wagon. A nest of blankets and cushions was ready for me. I was surprised that Jacob included me in the trip to Hebron. Bilhah and Zilpah rode in a second wagon. His sons rode the strong donkeys brought from Egypt.

"The family that God gave me in Haran will go with me to Hebron. We will give thanks to the One God and pray for safe travel to Egypt." My husband's words explained the arrangement. "The flocks and the rest of the tribe will remain at Beersheba and prepare for the trip."

Simeon took up the reins and set the wagon in motion. I asked my son about his time in Egypt. "The jail was not really a bad place," he remarked. "The food was decent, but I missed being outside. Most of all I longed for my brothers. I was never so happy as when the guard opened the door. The Lord Governor's own personal bodyguard stood there. In rough Hebrew, he ordered me to follow him. I was ordered to bathe and trim my beard." As an aside he added, "The Egyptians are very strict about bathing regularly. You would not believe the bathing place. It was a room with water flowing from the wall into a pool." He looked at me with a grin. "Mother, the paintings on the walls were of men and women bathing together." He laughed outright at my exclamation of shock. "Don't worry, I didn't look, much."

It was good to hear him teasing me. I smiled up at this man whose absence caused such changes in my relationship with Jacob. "Tell me more," I urged.

"When I was dressed, the bodyguard led me through the palace but not to the audience chamber where we were all before. He took me to the private apartments of the Governor. The magnificence took my breath away. The paintings and the gold and ebony carvings, oh, wait until you see them, Mother!" He shrugged to indicate that he could not describe such wonders. "The guard opened one of the doors. My brothers were seated at a low table. We embraced and I saw Benjamin. He was walking around the room staring at each item. There was another small table set on a low dais next to a chair with lion feet."

"Real paws?" I asked in surprise.

Again he flashed a warmsmile. "No, carved from the wood, but so realistic you would have thought that they could come to life and spring on you. The steward came in and showed us to our places around the table. We didn't understand how he could know our birth order. Reuben sat first at the head of the table, then me and so on around the table, ending with Benjamin who sat across from Reuben."

"Joseph would know that," I mused.

"True, but we didn't know that the man was our brother. He came into the room and immediately left. We thought the Lord Governor was angered. 'What shall we do?' we asked each other. Egyptians with spears stood inside and outside the doors so escape seemed hopeless. We were still discussing what to do when the man reappeared. He asked about Father and examined Benjamin closely. Reuben and Judah had a trunk with gifts that they presented to the Governor. They also explained that they brought back the silver for the first purchase that had been found in their bags of grain. 'Here is a double portion for more grain,' Judah said. The man waved it off. 'I was paid last time. Perhaps your God returned your silver.' Then he ordered the food to be brought." Simeon licked his lips at the memory. "Egypt has fared well, even in the famine. We had fowl and mutton. There were fruits and vegetables as well as several breads. It was a magnificent feast."

"When did you learn that the Governor is Joseph?" I wanted to know.

"Not at that meal. Although he did speak to us in our own language, we never suspected. We believed it when he told us he had learned many languages to deal with emissaries from various countries. We did wonder why he was so interested in our families. He asked about our wives and children. The fact that even Benjamin was a father seemed to amaze him."

"When he left, Benjamin was a child. It must have been surprising to see him grown and a father," I mused aloud.

"After the meal, the Governor sent us to the storehouse with a servant boy as guide. We set out for home with our donkeys loaded with two sacks each."

Jacob rode up on a donkey to say, "We will make camp just over the hill. There is some water and a little grass for the night."

The long day's ride had stiffened my joints. For a moment, I feared I could not move. Simeon helped me from the wagon. Slowly and stiffly, I moved toward the tent. I pretended to eat, but my heart was too full of fear and guilt. God had taken even my hatred and worked a blessing for Jacob, but what penalty would he demand from me?

Reuben lifted me into my cozy pillow and goatskin-lined bed in the wagon before the sun was up in the morning. After he carefully wrapped the blanket around me against the morning chill and we were rolling north, I spoke to my oldest son. "Tell me more of how you learned of Joseph. Simeon told me how you left Egypt with loaded donkeys. How did you come here with these wagons and oxen?"

A grim look came into Reuben's eyes. "Leaving Egypt wasn't that easy. We had barely left the town and reached the open road when we heard the thunder of hooves and chariot wheels. Thinking it was some important person on a journey, we drew the animals off the road so they could pass." He shuddered at the memory. "It was the Lord Governor's guard and steward in the chariot. A troop of soldiers surrounded us with drawn swords." Reuben ran his hand through his hair. "Then the steward made the strangest accusation. 'One of you has stolen the Lord Zaphenath-Paneah's goblet. It is the cup he drinks from and that he uses to pour out the morning offering.' "

"Why?" I couldn't stop the question. "If the Governor is Joseph, why would he say such a thing?"

"It was a test to see if we'd sell out another brother to be a slave in Egypt." Reuben hung his head. "I suppose he wanted to see if we'd save our hides like we did a year ago when we left Simeon. Maybe he wanted to see if we hated Benjamin as much as we hated him."

"What did you do?" I leaned forward ignoring the swirling in my head.

"The Governor's bodyguard and soldiers searched our bags and found the silver goblet in Benjamin's sack. They tied him and shoved him onto the floor of the chariot. In a cloud of dust they headed back to the city. The steward's parting words, 'This man will pay the penalty for such treachery. He will be Lord Governor, Zaphenath-Paneah's slave' rang in our ears. Desperately we ran after them, dragging the donkeys by their halters. I'm sure the brays of complaint could be heard for miles." My son allowed himself to smile. "When we reached the palace we had to beg for entrance. The Governor's bodyguard finally came and ordered us to follow him. He took us to the huge audience chamber where we first saw the Governor."

"Benjamin?" I asked breathlessly.

"Yes, he was there. Two Egyptian soldiers stood guard and he was still bound. He was very frightened. We tried to comfort him and Judah assured him that all would be well. Looking around at the spears in the hands of the guards by the doors it was hard to believe that."

I sank back with a sigh of relief onto my pillows. My sons had in the end supported their brother. Surely God would not punish them.

"Rest, my mother," Reuben urged hearing my sigh. "We will talk more later."

That night I lay in the tent staring at the stars. I thought about the long journey of my life. Memories of raising Rachel, marrying Jacob, and hating my sister because he loved her beauty floated in my mind. Regret for the jealous sickness that spread to my sons and led to Joseph's exile and my husband's grief led to tears. My heart was humbled as I marveled at the power of Jacob's God in raising a Hebrew to power in Egypt. I rejoiced that the One God had restored his beloved son to my husband. In the stillness of the night I knew that Joseph's restoration was proof that I was forgiven.

"Out of my enviousness, you have brought deliverance for your servant Jacob and all his family." With awe in my heart I prayed. "I see that you love me even though I have been so foolish. You have taken my mistakes and doubts and turned them into blessing. God of my husband, you are not bound by borders and even human failure doesn't stop you. My God, I see now that your hand has been on me all my life. I have wasted it repining for what I thought I wanted. All along, you gave me what I really needed. You have blessed me with my sons and with my wise husband. Continue your blessings on Jacob."

Lying weakly on my bed, I felt a peace in my heart that I never expected. The love of the One God enveloped me like a blanket. I let the feeling seep into my bones. Finally, I slept secure in the knowledge that the One God would indeed be with us wherever we were. My dreams were not troubled.

In the morning, I insisted that I was better and even swallowed the bread and thinned wine that Zilpah brought me. Judah bundled me into the wagon. "We will be at Hebron today," he remarked climbing up to drive the wagon.

I looked at the son I had named "praise", even though I felt no joy in my heart when he was born. Today I felt filled with adoration of the God who was now the God I claimed as my own. "Simeon and Reuben have told me part of how you learned that the Lord Governor of Egypt is your lost brother, Joseph. Tell me the rest." I urged my son as we settled into a steady pace.

He smiled fondly at me. "My mother, you are always curious. What have they told you?"

"Simeon told how you all ate with the Governor and didn't recognize him."

"No." The tall man shook his head. "He is a prince in Egypt. He wears Egyptian clothing, his eyes are painted and the crown covered his head. How could we have suspected that he was our brother?"

"Reuben told me how Benjamin was arrested and that you all raced back to the city dragging the donkeys." I smiled at the image in my mind and Judah answered with a grin.

"We probably looked foolish dragging those stupid beasts. We were pushing and pulling. They were kicking and hauling on their harnesses. Issachar even put his shoulder under one donkey's rump and rushed it forward on its front legs. We were frantic." Then he continued more seriously, "We all knew how fearful Father was to let Benjamin go with us at all. I remembered his words, 'If my son dies, I, too, will die.'

None of us dared return without our brother. We were of one mind as we stormed the palace. The guards didn't want to let us past. They kept pointing to the full sacks on the donkeys and pointing out of the city. I suppose they thought we were greedy and wanted more than our share. Not one of them understood our shouted demands to see the Governor. At last the Governor's personal guard arrived."

Judah sheepishly smiled, "My relief at having someone who could understand me was so intense that I blurted out, 'We have come to save our brother.' "

I laughed, "What did he say to that?"

"He gave me an odd look," Judah acknowledged, "but he led us into the palace. He took us to the audience chamber. There was Benjamin bound and on his knees. We rushed to him but the spears prevented us from embracing him. All around the room Egyptian soldiers held their posts with expressionless faces. 'This is all a mistake,' I told my brothers. 'We must trust in the God of our father. Only he can help us now.' "

Surprised at the words from my self-sufficient son, I tilted my head to look at him more fully.

"Yes, Mother, I prayed," he replied, seeing my look.

"Then the Lord Governor Zaphenath-Paneah came in. He and his attendants strode straight across the room. We scattered and fell on our faces before him. When he reached the dais he turned with that cursed cup in his hand. All he said was 'Well.' " Judah paused and seemed to gather himself together. "I forced myself to rise to my knees to beg for mercy. 'The boy is innocent.' My words seemed to fall on deaf ears. 'Our father will die if the boy doesn't return with us.' I thought I saw the man flinch, but he stared implacably at us. Finally I cried out, 'Take me as your slave in his stead. Only let the boy return to his father.' All my brothers joined in offering themselves in Benjamin's place."

I wiped away a tear. Judah rubbed his forehead. He was reliving the intensity of the eternity before the Lord Governor of Egypt.

"We were terrified," he confessed, "but we were united in saving Benjamin and sending him home to our father."

"My son," I whispered, "God is merciful and gracious."

"Yes," the man agreed, "for suddenly the Governor ordered all Egyptians out of the room. We cowered away from him when he stepped off the dais. With our eyes averted, we waited for him to pass judgment. Instead of anger, there was sorrow in his voice when he spoke."

Another tear slid down my cheek and a matching tear disappeared into my son's beard.

"What did he say?" I barely breathed as I waited for the answer. How had Joseph revealed himself to his brothers after all these years?

Gazing at the nearby hills, my son recalled, "'Don't you recognize me?' That's what he said." Taking a deep breath, Judah continued, "Then he took off his headdress and said, 'It is I, Joseph.' He stood there in the middle of us all. We were all too afraid to glance at him. 'Look at me,' he ordered. Half afraid, I lifted my head." In a gesture of agitation, my son ran his hand over his face and beard. "There stood the Lord Governor, but he was Joseph. I looked up into those eyes that are like my Aunt Rachel's. Benjamin has them, too."

"You must have been terrified," I murmured, almost afraid to interrupt.

The broad shoulders heaved in a sigh. "We were. I remembered the fear and rage in those brown eyes as the slave trader dragged him away. I heard again his pleas and remembered Father's grief when we gave him the bloodied coat. Speechless, I fell flat on the floor at his feet." He shook his head as he went on. "Joseph spoke softly and with tears, 'Don't be afraid. I mean you no harm. What you meant for evil, the One God of our father meant for good. He sent me here to save our family in this famine.' Finally, he convinced us all to quit groveling. Somewhat hesitant, we hugged our brother. Except Benjamin, who was ecstatic and grinning from ear to ear. The revelation that his brother was alive totally erased his fear of the Lord Governor."

"There was no punishment then?"

"No one stole anything." Judah smiled ruefully. "It was Joseph's test of our honesty and faithfulness."

"Then what happened?" I sought to hear the rest of the story for I saw the hills around Hebron drawing nearer with each turn of the wheels. In the morning, Jacob could offer his sacrifices. Dinah and her family would join us when we moved south again. We would all live in Egypt for the rest of the famine time.

Briefly he concluded, "Joseph took us to his apartments. We met his wife and two sons. In the morning he went with us a day's journey. He sent all the wagons and provisions and servants to help us. 'Tell my father that Joseph is alive. Come to live in Egypt for there are five more years of famine still to come.' Still stunned by all that happened, we left the Black Land and came to our father. The rest you know."

Amazed at the saga, I rested in the soft pillows and blankets as the cart rolled northward. I marveled at how Joseph, sold as a slave over twenty years before, had become a ruler in Egypt. "Only by your hand, my God, could such a thing happen. I see that your hand has been on Joseph and on Jacob since the beginning. You do not fail in your promises. Indeed, You singled out Jacob, and you have made him a great nation and surely you will again bring him to this land that you promised to Abraham the Wanderer and his descendants forever."

I fell into a doze and awakened in my bed. Zilpah and Bilhah were beside me. My head felt heavy and I wondered where we were. I remember thinking that I needed to find Rachel and tell her something. I moved my hand and Zilpah took it in her own.

"Mistress," she said, and I saw concern in her eyes.

Bilhah held a cup to my lips. Then I saw Dinah and remembered everything.

"God has blessed Jacob," I whispered. "Everyone must be told."

# Epilogue

The old woman looked around at her sons. Tears glistened in their eyes. "For too long, I raged against Rachel and against Jacob for not loving me," she said. I wanted them to love me for being beautiful. Too late I have learned and understand that they loved me for who I am."

Jacob bent his head to kiss his wife's forehead. "You are my faithful Leah. You are the strength of the family," he whispered.

She seemed almost beautiful as she smiled softly up at the man. "My husband, God is your strength. He will be with you to bring you to Egypt and back. Your God always keeps his promises." Turning her head, she admonished the eleven men still crouched near the bed. "My sons, you are all my sons, though I didn't bear you all. I have raised you and watched you grow into good men, true husbands, and loving fathers. Do not forget the God of Israel, your father, when you are in Egypt. Remember and teach your children how He showed grace by redeeming your anger and restoring your brother to you. Joseph has forgiven you. Accept that gift. My God has forgiven you as he has forgiven me. Do not be afraid. Trust in the God of Abraham, Isaac, and Jacob. He has promised to bring you back to this land as a mighty nation. Let go of the remaining fear and grudges against your brother. Do not continue to blame yourselves. The mighty hand of God has turned our evil designs and anger to great good for all."

Lying back, the woman closed her eyes. A slight smile slid across her lips as a breath sighed, "Rachel, Rachel, I must tell ..."

Jacob heard the softly spoken words fade. "No!" The cry wrenched from him in agony as he gathered his wife close. Unashamed, he wept. Zilpah and Bilhah raised the mourning cry. Dinah fell across her mother's lap wailing and her brothers took up the keening through their tears. Throughout the camp, each person added a voice to the lament.

"We will bury Leah in the cave where Abraham and Sarah and my parents are buried," Jacob instructed his sons in the morning. He looked very old, and the men glanced at each other in concern. "Leah, my beloved, here next to Abraham and his cherished Sarah you will rest. As Isaac and Rebekah are side by side, so shall I return to be buried beside you, my faithful Leah. My dearest wife, you reminded me of the faithfulness of the One God by your words and deeds. I will go to Egypt, but my joy in Joseph is less for I am without you." Jacob's words were spoken through tears as he laid his hand on hers for the last time before leaving the cave.

The days of mourning ended and the caravan faced southward toward Egypt. The mood was sorrowful as sons and family missed the gentle hand of the woman. For so many years, she had been the inspiration of the tribe. Jacob was not the only one who missed her guidance and love. Dinah divided her days between her family and her father. Like her brothers, she missed the encouragement of her mother even as she took over the duties of overseeing the camp.

Gradually, however, the excitement of reaching Egypt and seeing Joseph again began to occupy everyone's thoughts. "I will see my son," Jacob told his sons daily. Ten of the men wondered if their half-brother would turn on them after the family was safely settled in Egypt. "We must not be tempted by the ways and gods of this land," the old man warned his sons. "The children must learn all that the God of our fathers has done. They must learn of the blessings and promises given to Abraham and to my father Isaac and to me." Levi nodded when Jacob added, "As my beloved Leah said, 'God is gracious and has blessed me fully throughout my life.' The One God will be with us in Egypt, and like Abraham the Wanderer, we will return to Canaan a great nation."